THE JEWE~~LS OF AP~~TOR

Fate brought them together to serve the will of the Goddess Argo incarnate:

SNAKE—A little four-armed thief, mute and telepathic, who understands the secret of the mystic jewels they seek.

URSON—Huge, bearlike, cursed, a sailor accused of murder and worse. Chosen for a terrible purpose.

GEO—Poet, scholar and decipherer of ancient mysteries, whose part in the quest alters him forever.

Shipmates on a voyage through fog-bound seas, through treacherous jungles, abandoned cities and decaying temples filled with half-human creatures, they seek the prize in an age-old war between a primal god and goddess, the legacy of an earlier age before the Great Fire.

Samuel R. Delany's first novel,
filled with rich poetry and vivid imagery.

Bantam Science Fiction and Fantasy Books
Ask your bookseller for the books you have missed

ALAS, BABYLON by Pat Frank
BABEL-17 by Samuel R. Delany
THE BEGINNING PLACE by Ursula Le Guin
A CANTICLE FOR LEIBOWITZ by Walter Miller, Jr.
CENTURY'S END by Russell M. Griffin
DHALGREN by Samuel R. Delany
DRAGON LENSMAN by David A. Kyle
THE EINSTEIN INTERSECTION by Samuel R. Delany
FANTASTIC VOYAGE by Isaac Asimov
THE GATES OF HEAVEN by Paul Preuss
GOSH! WOW! edited by Forrest J. Ackerman
HELLSTROM'S HIVE by Frank Herbert
THE HEROES OF ZARA KEEP by Guy Gregory
HONEYMOON IN HELL by Fredric Brown
THE HUMANOID TOUCH by Jack Williamson
JEM by Frederik Pohl
THE JEWELS OF APTOR by Samuel R. Delany
A LIFE IN THE DAY OF . . . AND OTHER SHORT STORIES
  by Frank Robinson
LORD VALENTINE'S CASTLE by Robert Silverberg
MAN PLUS by Frederik Pohl
MATHEW SWAIN: HOT TIME IN OLD TOWN by Mike McQuay
MOCKINGBIRD by Walter Trevis
NOVA by Samuel R. Delany
QUAS STARBRITE by James R. Berry
SLOW TO FALL DAWN by Stephen Leigh
SONG OF SORCERY by Elizabeth Scarborough
STEEL OF RAITHSKAR by Randall Garrett and Vicki Ann Heydron
A STORM UPON ULSTER by Kenneth Flint
SUNDIVER by David Brin
TALES OF NEVERYON by Samuel R. Delany
TIME STORM by Gordon Dickson
TRITON by Samuel R. Delany
THE WINDHOVER TAPES: AN IMAGE OF VOICES
  by Warren C. Norwood

THE JEWELS
OF
APTOR

Samuel R. Delany

BANTAM BOOKS
TORONTO · NEW YORK · LONDON · SYDNEY

THE JEWELS OF APTOR

A Bantam book / published by arrangement with the author

PRINTING HISTORY

First published in Great Britain in 1968 by Victor Gollancz Ltd.
Bantam edition / June 1982

ISBN 0-553-20311-8

Published simultaneously in the United States and Canada

Bantam Books are published by Bantam Books, Inc. Its trademark, consisting of the words ''Bantam Books'' and the portrayal of a rooster is Registered in U.S. Patent and Trademark Office and in other countries. Marca Registrada. Bantam Books, Inc., 666 Fifth Avenue, New York, New York 10103.

PRINTED IN THE UNITED STATES OF AMERICA

0 9 8 7 6 5 4 3 2 1

The waves flung up against the purple glow
of double sleeplessness. Along the piers
the ships return; but sailing I would go
through double rings of fire, double fears.
So therefore let your bright vaults heave the night
about with ropes of wind and points of light
and say, as all the rolling stars go, "I
have stood my feet on rock and seen the sky."

The opening lines of the epic
of the conflicts between Leptar and Aptor,
by the one-armed poet Geo

THE JEWELS
OF
APTOR

Afterwards, she was taken down to the sea.

She didn't feel too well, so she sat on a rock and scrunched her toes in the wet sand. She looked across the water, hunched her shoulders a little. "I think it was pretty awful. I think it was terrible. Why did you show it to me? He was just a little boy. What reason could they possibly have had for doing that to him?"

"It was just a film. We showed it to you so that you would learn."

"But it was a film of something that really happened!"

"It happened several years ago, several hundred miles away."

"But it *did* happen; you used a tight beam to spy on them and when the image came in on the vision screen, you made a film of it, and—Why did you show it to me?"

"What have we been teaching you?"

But she couldn't think: only the picture in her mind, vivid movements, scarlets, bright agony. "He was just a child," she said. "He couldn't have been more than eleven or twelve."

"*You* are a child. You aren't sixteen yet."

"What was I supposed to learn?"

"Look around. You should see something."

But it was still too vivid, too red, too bright. . . .

"You should be able to learn it right here on this beach, in the trees back there, in the rocks down here, in the shells around your feet. You do see it; you don't recognize it." His voice brightened. "Actually you're a very fine student. You learn quickly. Do you remember anything from your study of telepathy a month ago?''

" 'By a method similar to radio broadcast and reception,' '' she recited, " 'the synapse patterns of conscious thought are read from one cranial cortex and duplicated in another, resulting in a duplication of sensory impressions experienced—' But I can't do it; so it doesn't help *me*!''

"What about history, then? You did extremely well in the examination. Does knowing about all the happenings in the world before and after the Great Fire help you?''

"Well. It's . . . it's interesting.''

"The film you saw was, in a way, history. That is, it happened in the past.''

"But it was so—'' Her eyes beat before the flashing waves —"horrible!''

"Does history fascinate you only because it's interesting? Don't you ever want to know the reason behind some of the things those people do in your books?''

"Yes, I want to know the reasons! I want to know the reason they nailed that man to the oaken cross. I want to know why they did that to him.''

"A good question . . . Which reminds me: at about the same time they were nailing him to that cross, it was decided in China that the forces of the Universe were to be represented by a circle, half black, half white. To remind themselves, however, that there is no pure force, no single and unique reason, they put a spot of white paint in the black half and a spot of black paint in the white. Interesting?''

She frowned, wondering at the transition. But he was going on:

"And do you remember the goldsmith, the lover, how he recorded in his autobiography that at age four, he and his father saw the Fabulous Salamander on their hearth by the fire; and his father smacked the boy across the room into a rack of kettles, saying something to the effect that little Cellini was too young to remember the incident unless it was accompanied by pain.''

"I remember the story,'' she said. "And I remember Cellini said he wasn't sure if the smack was the reason he remembered the Salamander or the Salamander the reason he remembered the smack.''

"Yes, yes!" he cried. "That's it. The reason, the reasons..." In his excitement, his hood fell back and she saw his face in the late afternoon's copper light. "Don't you see the pattern?"

Scored forehead, the webbing at his eyes: she traced the pattern of age there, and let her eyes drop. "Only I don't know what a Salamander is."

"It's like the blue lizards that sing outside your window," he explained. "Only it isn't blue, and it doesn't sing."

"Then why should anyone want to remember it?" She grinned. But he was not looking at her.

"And the painter," he was saying, "you remember, in Florence. He was painting a picture of La Gioconda. As a matter of fact, he had to take time from the already crumbling picture of the Last Supper of the man who was nailed to the cross of oak to paint her. And he put a smile on her face of which men asked for centuries, 'What is the reason she smiles so strangely?' Yes, the reason, don't you see? Just look around."

"What about the Great Fire?" she asked. "When they dropped flames from the skies and the harbors boiled; that was reasonless. That was like what they did to that boy."

"Oh, no," he said to her. "Not reasonless. True, when the Great Fire came, people all over the earth screamed, 'Why? Why? How can man do this to man? What is the reason?' But just look around you, right here! On the beach!"

"I guess I can't see it yet," she said. "I can just see what they did to him, and it was awful."

"Well." He pulled together his robe. "Perhaps when you stop seeing what they did so vividly, you will start seeing why they did it. I think it's time for us to go back now."

She slid off the rock and started walking beside him, barefoot in the sand. "That boy...I wasn't sure, he was all tied up; but he had four arms, didn't he?"

"He did."

She shuddered again. "You know, I can't just go around just saying it was awful. I think I'm going to write a poem. Or make something. Or both. I've got to get it out of my head."

"That wouldn't be a bad idea," he mumbled as they approached the trees in front of the river. "Not bad at all."

And several days later, several hundred miles away...

CHAPTER ONE

Waves flung themselves at the blue evening. Low light burned on the wet ships that slipped by mossy pilings into the docks as water sloshed at the city's rotten stones.

Gangplanks, chained to wooden pullies, scraped into place on concrete blocks; and the crew, after the slow Captain and the tall Mate, loped raffishly along the boards which sagged with the pounding of bare feet. In bawling groups, pairs, or singly, they howled into the waterfront streets, by the yellow light from inn doors, the purple portals leading to rooms full of smoke and the stench of burnt poppies, laughter and the sheen on red lips, to the houses of women.

The Captain, with eyes the color of sea under fog, touched his sword hilt with his fist and said quietly, "Well, they've gone. We better start collecting new sailors for the ten we lost at Aptor. Ten good men, Jordde. I get ill when I think of the bone and broken meat they became."

"Ten for the dead," sneered the Mate, "and twenty for the living we'll never see again. Any sailor that would want to continue this trip with us is crazy. We'll do well if we only lose twenty." He was a wire bound man, on whom any clothing looked baggy.

"I'll never forgive her for ordering us to that monstrous Island," said the Captain.

"I wouldn't speak too loudly," mumbled the Mate. "Yours isn't to forgive her. Besides, she went with them, and was in as much danger as they were. It's only luck she came back."

Suddenly the Captain asked, "Do you believe the stories of magic they tell of her?"

"Why, sir?" asked the Mate. "Do you?"

"No, I don't." The Captain's certainty came too quickly. "Still, with three survivors out of thirteen, that she should be among them, with hardly a robe torn . . ."

"Perhaps they wouldn't touch a woman," suggested Jordde.

"Perhaps," said the Captain.

"And she's been strange ever since then. She walks at night. I've seen her going by the rails, looking from the seafire to the stars, and back."

"Ten good men," mused the Captain. "Hacked up, torn in bits. I wouldn't have believed that much barbarity in the world, if I hadn't seen that arm, floating on the water. It even chills me now, the way the men ran to the rail, pointed at it. And it just raised itself up, like a sign, then sank in a wash of foam and green water."

"Well," said the Mate, "we have men to get."

"I wonder if she'll come ashore?"

"She'll come if she wants, Captain. Her doing is no concern of yours. Your job is the ship and to do what she asks."

"I have more of a job than that," and he looked back at his still craft.

The Mate touched the Captain's shoulder. "If you're going to speak things like that, speak them softly, and only to me."

"I have more of a job than that," the Captain repeated. Then, suddenly, he started away; the Mate followed him down the darkening dockside.

The wharf was still a moment. Then a barrel toppled from a pile of barrels, and a figure moved like a bird's shadow between two mounds of cargo.

At the same time two men approached down a street filled with the day's last light. The bigger one threw a great shadow that aped his gesticulating arms on the crowded buildings. His bare feet slapped the cobbles like halved hams. His shins were bound with thongs and pelts. He waved one hand in explanation and rubbed the back of the other on his short, mahogany beard. "You're going to ship out, eh friend? You think they'll take your rhymes and jingles instead of muscles and rope pulling?"

The smaller, in a white tunic looped with a leather belt, laughed in spite of his friend's ranting. "Fifteen minutes ago you thought it was a fine idea, Urson. You said it would make me a man."

"Oh, it's a life to make——" Urson's hand went up—— "and it's a life to break men." It fell.

The slighter one pushed back black hair from his forehead, stopped, and looked at the boats. "You still haven't told me why no ship has taken you on in the past three months." Absently, he followed the rigging, like black slashes in blue silk. "A year ago I'd never see you in for more than three days at once."

The gesticulating arm suddenly encircled the smaller man's waist and lifted a leather pouch from the belt. "Are you sure, friend Geo," began the giant, "that we couldn't use up some of this silver on wine before we go. If you want to do this right, then right is how it should be done. When you sign up on a ship you're supposed to be broke and tight. It shows you're capable of getting along without the inconvenience of money and can hold your liquor."

"Urson, get your paw off!" Geo pulled the purse away.

"Now here," countered Urson, reaching for it once more, "you don't have to grab."

"Look, I've kept you drunk five nights now; it's time to sober up. Suppose they don't take us, who's going——" But Urson, laughing, made another swipe.

Geo leaped back with the purse. "Now cut that out——" In leaping, his feet struck the fallen barrel. He fell backwards to the wet cobbles. The pouch splattered away, jingling.

They scrambled——

Then the bird's shadow darted between the cargo piles; the slight figure bounded forward, swept the purse up with one hand, pushed himself away from the pile of crates with another; and there were two more pumping at his side as he ran.

"What the devil . . ." began Urson, and then: "What the *devil*!"

"Hey you!" Geo lurched to his feet. "Come back!"

Urson had already loped a couple of steps after the fleeing quadrabrad, now halfway down the block.

Then, like a wineglass stem snapping, a voice: "Stop, little thief. Stop."

He stopped as though he had hit a wall.

"Come back, now. Come back."

He turned, and docilely started back, his movements, so lithe a moment ago, mechanical now.

"It's just a kid," Urson said.

He was a dark-haired boy, naked except for a ragged breech. He was staring fixedly beyond them. And he had four arms.

Now they turned and looked also.

She stood on the ship's gangplank, dark against what sun still washed the horizon. One hand held something close at her throat, and wind, snagging a veil, held the purple gauze against the red swath at the world's edge, then dropped it.

The boy, automaton, approached her.

"Give it to me, little thief."

He handed her the purse. She took it. Then she dropped her other hand from her neck. The moment she did so, the boy staggered backwards, turned, and ran straight into Urson, who said, "Ooof," and then, "God damned spider!"

The boy struggled like a hydra in furious silence. Urson held. "You stick around . . . Owww! . . . to get yourself thrashed . . . there." Urson locked one arm across the boy's chest. With his other hand he caught all four wrists; he lifted up, hard. The thin body shook like wires jerked taut, but the boy was still silent.

Now the woman came across the dock. "This belongs to you, gentlemen?" she asked, extending the purse.

"Thank you, ma'am," grunted Urson, reaching forward.

"I'll take that, ma'am," said Geo, intercepting. Then he recited:

> *"Shadows melt in light of sacred laughter.*
> *Hands and houses shall be one hereafter."*

"Thank you," he added.

Beneath the veil her eyebrows raised. "You have been schooled in courtly rites? Are you perhaps a student at the University?"

Geo smiled. "I was, until a short time ago. But funds are low and I have to get through the summer somehow. I'm going to sea."

"Honorable, but perhaps foolish."

"I am a poet, ma'am; they say poets are fools. Besides, my friend here says the sea will make a man of me. To be a good poet, one must be a good man."

"More honorable, less foolish. What sort of man is your friend?"

"My name is Urson." The giant stepped up. "And I've been the best hand on any ship I've sailed on."

"Urson? The Bear? I thought bears did not like water. Except polar bears. It makes them mad. I believe there was an old spell, in antiquity, for taming angry bears...."

"Calmly, brother bear," Geo began to recite:

> *"calm the winter sleep.*
> *Fire shall not harm*
> *water not alarm.*
> *While the current grows,*
> *amber honey flows,*
> *golden salmon leap."*

"Hey," said Urson. "I'm not a bear!"

"Your name means bear," Geo said. Then to the lady, "You see I have been well trained."

"I'm afraid I have not," she replied. "Poetry and rituals were a hobby of a year's passing interest when I was younger. But that was all." Now she looked down at the four-armed boy. "You two look alike. Dark eyes, dark hair." She laughed. "Are there other things in common between poets and thieves?"

"Well," complained Urson with a jerk of his chin, "this one here won't spare a few silvers for a drink of good wine to wet his best friend's throat, and that's a sort of thievery if you ask me."

"I did not ask," said the woman.

Urson huffed.

"Little thief," the woman said. "Little Four Arms. What is your name?"

Silence, and the dark eyes narrowed.

"I can make you tell me," and she raised her hand to her throat again.

Now the eyes opened wide and the boy pushed back against Urson's belly.

Geo reached toward the boy's neck where a ceramic disk hung from a leather thong. Glazed on the white enamel was a wriggle of black with a small dot of green for an eye at one end. "This will do for a name," Geo said.

"The Snake?" She dropped her threatening hand. "How good a thief are you?" She looked at Urson. "Let him go."

"And miss thrashing his little backside—?"

"He will not run away."

Urson released him.

Four hands came from behind the boy's back and began massaging one another's wrists. The dark eyes watched her as she repeated: "How good a thief are you?"

Suddenly he reached into his clout and drew out what seemed another thong similar to the one around his neck. He held up the fist, the fingers opened slowly to a cage.

"What is it?" Urson peered over Snake's shoulder.

The woman leaned forward, then suddenly straightened. "You . . ." she began.

Snake's fist closed like a sea-polyp.

"You are a fine thief indeed."

"What is it?" Urson asked. "I didn't see anything."

"Show them," she said.

Snake opened his hand. On the dirty palm, in coiled leather, held by a clumsy wire cage was a milky sphere the size of a man's eye.

"A very fine thief," repeated the woman in a voice dulled strangely from its previous brittle clarity. She had pulled her veil aside now; Geo saw, where her hand had again raised to her throat, the tips of her slim fingers held an identical jewel; only this one, in a platinum claw, hung from a wrought gold chain.

Her eyes, unveiled, raised to meet Geo's. A slight smile lifted her lips. "No," she said. "Not quite so clever as I thought. At first I believed he had taken mine. But clever enough. You, schooled in the antiquity of Leptar's rituals, can you tell me what these baubles mean?"

Geo shook his head.

A breath suspired her pale mouth, and though her eyes still fixed his, she seemed to draw away, blown into some past shadow by the sigh. "No," she said. "It has all been lost or destroyed by the old priests and priestesses, the old poets.

> *"Freeze the drop in the hand*
> *and break the earth with singing.*
> *Hail the height of a man*
> *also the height of a woman.*
> *The eyes have imprisioned a vision. . . ."*

"She spoke the lines reverently. "Do you recognize any of this? Can you tell me where they are from?"

"Only one stanza of it," said Geo. "And that in a slightly different form." He recited:

> *"Burn the grain speck in the hand*
> *and batter the stars with singing.*
> *Hail the height of a man,*
> *also the height of a woman."*

"Well." She looked surprised. "You have done better than all the priests and priestesses of Leptar. What about this fragment? Where is it from?"

"It is a stanza of the discarded rituals of the Goddess Argo, the ones banned and destroyed five hundred years ago. The rest of the poem is completely lost," explained Geo. "Your priests and priestesses would not be aware of it, very likely. I discovered that stanza when I peeled away the binding paper of an ancient tome that I found in the Antiquity Collection in the Temple Library at Acedia. Apparently a page from an even older book had been used in the binding of this one. That is the only way it survived. I assume these are fragments of the rituals before Leptar purged her litanies. I know at least my variant stanza belongs to that period. Perhaps you have received a misquoted rendition; I will vouch for the authenticity of mine."

"No," she said, regretfully. "*Mine* is the authentic version. So, you too, are not that clever." She turned back to the boy. "But I have need of a good thief. Will you come with me? And you, Poet. I have need of one who thinks so meticulously and who delves into places where even my priests and priestesses cannot go. Will you come with me also?''

"Where are we going?"

"Aboard that ship." She smiled evasively toward the vessel.

"That's a good boat," said Urson. "I'd be proud to sail on her, Geo."

"The Captain is in my service," she told Geo. "He will take you on. Perhaps you will get a chance to see the world, and become the man you wish to be."

Geo saw Urson looking uneasy. "My friend goes on whatever ship I do. This we've promised each other. Besides, he is a good sailor, while I have no knowledge of the sea."

"On our last journey," the woman explained, "we lost men. I do not think your friend will have trouble getting a berth."

"Then we'll be honored to come," said Geo. "Under whose service shall we be, then, for we still don't know who you are?"

The veil fell across her face again. "I am a high priestess of the Goddess Argo. Now, who are you?"

"My name is Geo," Geo told her.

"I welcome you aboard our ship."

Just then, from down the street, came the Captain and Jordde. They walked slowly and heavily from the shadow that angled over the cables. The Captain squinted past the ships toward the horizon. Copper light filled the wrinkles and burnished the planes around his gray eyes. The Priestess turned to them. "Captain, I have three men as a token replacement for the ones my folly helped to lose."

Urson, Geo, and Snake frowned at each other, and then looked at the Captain.

Jordde shrugged. "You did almost as well as we did, ma'am."

"And the ones we did get . . ." The Captain shook his head. "Not the caliber of sailor I'd want for this sort of journey. Not at all."

"I'm a good sailor for any man's journey," Urson said, "though it be to the earth's end and back."

"You seem strong, a sea-bred man. But this one"—the Captain looked at Snake—"one of the Strange Ones . . ."

"They're bad luck on a ship," said the Mate. "Most ships won't take them at all, ma'am. This one's just a boy and, for all his spindles there, couldn't haul rope or reef sails. He'd be no good to us at all. And we've had too much bad luck already."

"He's not for rope pulling," explained the Priestess. "The little Snake is my guest. The others you can put to ship's work. I know you are short of men. But I have my own plans for this one."

"As you say, ma'am," said the Captain.

"But, Priestess—" began Jordde.

"As you say," repeated the Captain, and the Mate stepped back, quieted. The Captain turned to Geo now. "And who are you?"

"I'm Geo, before and still a poet. But I'll do what work you set me, sir."

"Today, young man, that's all I can ask of any sailor. You will find berths below. There are many vacant."

"And you?" Jordde asked Urson.

"I'm a good sea-son of the waves, can stand triple watch without flagging, and I believe I'm already hired." He looked to the Captain.

"What do they call you?" Jordde asked. "You have a familiar look, like one I've had under me before."

"They call me the handsome sailor, the fastest rope reeler, the quickest line hauler, the speediest reefer—"

"Your name, man, your name!"

"Some call me Urson."

"That's the name I knew you by before! But you had no beard then. Do you think I'd sail with you again, when I myself put it in black and white and sent it to every captain and mate in the dock? What sort of a crazy hawk would I be to pour poison like you into my forecastle? For three months now you've had no berth, and if you had none for three hundred years it would be too soon." Jordde turned to the Captain now. "He's a troublemaker, sir; he fights. Though he's wild as waves and with the strength of a mizzen spar; spirit in a man is one thing, and a tussle or two the same; but good sailor though he be, I've sworn not to have him on ship with me, sir. He's nearly murdered half a dozen men and probably murdered half a dozen more. No mate who knows the men of this harbor will take him on.''

The Priestess of Argo laughed. ''Captain, take him.'' She looked at Geo. ''The words for calming the angry bear have been recited before him. Now, Geo, we will see how good a poet you are, and if the spell works.'' At last she turned to Urson. ''Have you ever killed a man?''

Urson was silent a moment. ''I have.''

''Had you told me that,'' said the Priestess, ''I would have chosen you first. I have need of you also. Captain, you must take him. If he is a good sailor, then we cannot spare him. *I* will channel what special talents he may have. Geo, since you said the spell, and are his friend, I charge you with his control. Also, I wish to talk with you, Poet, student of rituals. Come. You all stay on shipboard tonight.''

She signaled them to follow, and they mounted the plank onto the deck. At the request to speak with Geo, Urson, Snake, and Jordde had exchanged glances; but now, as they crossed to the hatch, all were silent.

CHAPTER TWO

~~~~~~

An oil lamp leaked yellow light on the wooden walls. A mustiness of stale bedding lay around them as the three entered. Geo wrinkled his nose, then shrugged.

"Well," said Urson, "this is a pleasant enough hole." He climbed one of the tiers of bunked beds and pounded the ticking with the flat of his hand. "Here, I'll take this one. Wriggly-arms, you look like you have a strong stomach; you take the middle. And Geo, sling yourself down in the bottom there." He clumped to the floor. "The lower down you are," he explained, "the better you sleep, because of the rocking. Well, what do you think of your first forecastle?"

The poet was silent. Double pins of light struck yellow dots in his dark eyes, then went out as he turned from the lamp.

"I put you in the bottom because a little rough weather can unseat your belly pretty fast if you're up near the ceiling and not used to it," Urson expounded, dropping his hand heavily on Geo's shoulder. "I told you I'd look out for you, didn't I, friend?"

But Geo turned away and seemed to examine something else.

Urson looked at Snake, who was watching him from against the wall. Urson's glance was questioning. But Snake stayed silent.

"Hey," Urson called to Geo once more. "Let's you and me take a run around this ship and see what's tied down where. A good sailor does that first thing—unless he's too drunk. That lets the Captain and the Mate know he's got an alert eye out, and sometimes he can learn something that will ease some back-bending later on. What do you say—"

"Not now, Urson," interrupted Geo. "You go."

"Would you please tell me why my company suddenly isn't good enough for you. This silence is a bilgy way to treat somebody who's sworn himself to see that you make the best first voyage that a man could have. Why, I think—"

"When did you kill a man?"

Silence rumbled in the cabin, more palpable than the slosh of water outside. Urson stood still; his hands twisted to knots of bone and muscle. Then they opened. "Maybe it was a year ago," he said softly. "And maybe it was a year, two months, and five days, on a Thursday morning at eight o'clock in the brig of a heaving ship. Which would make it one year, two months, five days and ten hours, now."

"You killed a man? How could you go all this time and not tell me about it, then admit it to a stranger just like that. You were my friend; we've slept under the same blanket, drunk from the same wineskin. What sort of a person are you?"

"And what sort of a person are you?" asked the giant. "A nosy bastard that I'd break in seven pieces if . . ." He sucked in a breath. ". . . If I hadn't promised I'd make no trouble. I've never broken a promise to anyone, alive or dead." The fists formed, relaxed again.

"Urson, I didn't mean to judge you. Know that. But tell me about it. We've been like brothers; you can't keep a thing like that from . . ."

The heavy breathing continued. "You're so quick to tell me what I can or cannot do." Suddenly he raised one hand, flung it away, and spat on the floor. He turned toward the steps.

Then the noise hit. No; it was higher than sound. And it nearly broke their heads. Geo caught his ears, and whirled toward Snake. The boy's black eyes darted twin spots of light to Urson, to Geo, and back.

The noise came again, quieter this time, and recognizable as the word *help*. Only it was no sound; rather, the fading hum of a tuning fork rung inside their skulls, immediate, yet fuzzy.

you . . . help . . . me . . . together . . . came the words once more, indistinct and blurring into one another.

"Hey," Urson said, "is that you?"

do . . . not . . . angry . . . came the words.

"We're not angry," Geo said. "What are you doing?"

I . . . thinking . . . The words seemed to generate from the boy.

"What sort of a way to think is that if everyone can hear it?" demanded Urson.

Snake tried to explain: *not . . . everyone . . . just . . . you . . . you . . . think . . . I . . . hear . . .* came the soundless words. *I . . . think . . . you . . . hear . . .*

"I know we hear," Urson said. "It's just like you were talking."

"That's not what he means," Geo said. "He means he hears what we think just like we hear him. Is that right, Snake?"

when . . . you . . . think . . . loud . . . I . . . hear . . .

"I may just have been doing some pretty loud thinking," Urson said. "And if I thought something I wasn't supposed to, well, I apologize."

Snake didn't seem interested in the apology, but asked again: *you . . . help . . . me . . . together . . .*

"What sort of help do you want?" Geo asked.

"And what sort of trouble are you in that you need help out of it?" added Urson.

you . . . don't . . . have . . . good . . . minds . . . Snake said.

"What's that supposed to mean?" Urson asked. "Our minds are as good as any in Leptar. You heard the way the Priestess talked to my friend the poet, here."

"I think he means we don't hear very well," said Geo.

Snake nodded.

"Oh," Urson said. "Well, then you'll just have to go slow and be patient with us."

Snake shook his head: *mind . . . hoarse . . . when . . . shout . . . so . . . loud . . .* Suddenly he went over to the bunks. *you . . . hear . . . better . . . see . . . too . . . if . . . sleep . . .*

"Sleep is sort of far from me," Urson said, rubbing his beard with the back of his wrist.

"Me too," Geo admitted. "Can't you tell us something more?"

sleep . . . Snake said.

"What about talking like an ordinary human being?" suggested Urson, still somewhat perplexed.

once . . . speak . . . Snake told them.

"You say you could speak once?" asked Geo. "What happened?"

Here the boy opened his mouth and pointed.

Geo stepped forward, held the boy's chin in his hand, examined the face, and peered into the mouth. "By the Goddess!"

"What is it?" Urson asked.

Geo came away now, his face in a sickly frown. "His tongue has been hacked out," he told the giant. "And not too neatly."

"Who on the seven seas and six continents did a thing like that to you, boy?" Urson demanded.

Snake shook his head.

"Now come on, Snake," he urged. "You can't keep secrets like that from friends and expect them to rescue you from I don't know what. Now who was it hacked your voice away!"

what . . . man . . . you . . . kill . . . came the sound.

Urson stopped, and then he laughed. "All right," he said. "I see." His voice rose once more. "But if you can hear thoughts, you know the man already. And you know the reason. And this is what we'd find out of you, and only for help and friendship's sake."

you . . . know . . . the . . . man . . . Snake said.

Geo and Urson exchanged puzzled frowns.

sleep . . . said Snake. *you . . . sleep . . . now . . .*

Maybe we ought to try," said Geo, "and find out what's going on." He crossed to his bunk and slipped in. Urson hoisted himself onto the upper berth, dangling his feet against the wooden support. "It's going to be a long time before sleep gets to me tonight," he said. "You, Snake, little Strange One," he laughed. "Where do you people come from?" He glanced down at Geo. "You see them all around the city. Some with three eyes, some with one. You know, at Matra's House they say they keep a woman with eight breasts and two of something else." He laughed. "You know the rituals, know about magic. Aren't the Strange Ones some sort of magic?"

"The only mention of them in rituals says that they are ashes of the Great Fire. The Great Fire was back before the purges, the ones I spoke to the Priestess about, so I don't know anything more about them."

"Sailors have stories of the Great Fire," Urson said. "They say the sea boiled, great birds spat fire from the sky, and metal breasts rose up from the waves and destroyed the harbors. But what were the purges you mentioned?"

"About five hundred years ago," Geo explained, "all the rituals of the Goddess Argo were destroyed. A completely new set was initiated into the temple practices. All references to the earlier onces were destroyed also, and with them, much of Leptar's history. Stories have it that the rituals and incantations were too powerful. But this is just a guess, and most priests are very uncomfortable about speculating."

"That was after the Great Fire?" Urson asked.

"Nearly a thousand years after," Geo said.

"It must have been a great fire indeed if ashes from it are still falling from the wombs of healthy women." He looked down at Snake. "Is it true that a drop of your blood in vinegar will cure gout? If one of you kisses a female baby, will she have only girl children?" He laughed.

"You know those are only tales," Geo said.

"There used to be a short one with two heads that sat outside the Blue Tavern and spun a top all day. It was an idiot, though. But the dwarfs and the legless ones that wheel about the city and do tricks, they are clever. But strange, and quiet, usually."

"You oaf," chided Geo, "you could be one too. How many men do you know who reach our size and strength by normal means?"

"You're a crazy liar," said Urson. Then he scrunched his eyebrows together in thought, and at last shrugged. "Well, anyway, I never heard of one who could hear what you thought. It would make me uncomfortable walking down the street." He looked down at Snake between his legs. "Can you all do that?"

Snake, from the middle bunk, shook his head.

"That makes me feel better," said Urson. "Once we had one on a ship. Some captains will take them on. He had a little head, the size of my fist, or even smaller. But a great big chest, a huge man in every other way as well. And his eyes and nose and mouth and things weren't on that bald little knob, but on his chest, right here. One day he got into a fight, and got his head, if you could call it that, broke right in half with a marlin pin. Bleeding all over himself, he went down to the ship's surgeon, and came up an hour later with the whole thing cut off and a big bandage right where his neck should have been, and his big green eyes blinking out from under his collarbone." Urson stretched out on his back, but then suddenly looked over the edge of the berth toward Geo. "Hey, Geo, what about those little baubles she had. Do you know what they are?"

"No, I don't," Geo said. "But she was concerned over them enough." He looked up over the bunk bottom between himself and Urson. "Snake, will you give me another look at that thing again?"

Snake held out the thong and the jewel.

"Where did you get it?" Urson asked. "Oh never mind. I guess we learn that when we go to sleep."

Geo reached for it, but Snake's one hand closed and three others sprang around it. "I wasn't going to take it," explained Geo. "I just wanted to see."

Suddenly the door of the forecastle opened, and the tall Mate was silhouetted against the brighter light behind him. "Poet?" he called. "She wants to see you." Then he was gone.

Geo looked at the other two, shrugged, then swung off the berth, and made his way up the steps and into the hall.

On deck it was completely dark. Stars flecked the heaven, and the only thing to distinguish sea from sky was that the bottom half of the great sphere in which they seemed suspended was lightless. Light fell through a cabin window here, and another further on. Geo paused to look in the first, and then, on distinguishing nothing, went toward the second.

Halfway, a door before him opened and a blade of illumination sliced the deck. He jumped.

"Come in," summoned the Priestess of Argo. He turned into a windowless cabin and stopped one step beyond the threshold. The walls rippled tapestries, lucent green, scarlet. Golden braziers perched on tapering tripods beneath pale blue smoke that lent thin incense in the room, piercing faintly but cleanly into his nostrils like knives. Light lashed the polished wooden newels of a great bed on which silk, damasked satin, and brocade swirled. A huge desk, cornered with wooden eagles, was spread with papers, instruments of cartography, sextants, rules, compasses; great, shabby books were piled on one corner. From the beamed ceiling, hung by thick chains, swayed a branching petrolabra of oil cups, some in the hands of demons, or the mouths of monkeys, burning in the bellies of nymphs, or between the horns of satyrs' heads, red, clear green, or yellow.

"Come in," repeated the Priestess. "Close the door."

Geo obeyed.

She walked behind her desk, sat down, and folded her hands in front of her veiled face. "Poet," she said, "you have had moments to think. What do you make of this all? What can you tell me of this journey we are about to make that I shall not have to tell you?"

"Only that its importance must be of great concern to Leptar."

"Do you know just how great the concern is?" she asked. "It is great enough to jar every man, woman, and child in Leptar, from the highest priestess to the most deformed Strange One. The world of words and emotions and intellect has been your range till now, Poet. But what do you know of the real world, outside Leptar?"

"That there is much water, some land, and mostly ignorance."

"What tales have you heard from your bear friend, Urson? He is a traveled man and should know some of what there is of the earth."

"The stories of sailors," said Geo, "are menageries of beasts that no one has ever seen, of lands for which no maps exist, and of peoples no man has met."

She smiled. "Since I boarded this ship I have heard many tales from sailors, and I have learned more from them than from all my priests. You, on the docks this evening, have been the only man to give me another scrap of the puzzle except a few drunken seamen, misremembering old fantasies." She paused. "What do you know of the jewels you saw tonight?"

"Nothing, ma'am."

"A common thief hiding on the docks has one; I, a priestess of Argo, possess another; and if you had one, you would probably exchange it for a kiss with some tavern maid. What do you know of the god Hama?"

"I know of no such god."

"You," she said, "who can spout all the rituals and incantations of the White Goddess Argo, you do not even know the name of the Dark God Hama. What do you know of the Island of Aptor?"

"Nothing, ma'am."

"This boat has been to Aptor once and now will return. Ask your ignorant friend the Bear to tell you tales of Aptor; and blind, wise Poet, you will laugh, and probably he will too. But I will tell you: his tales, his legends, and his fantasies are not a tithe of the truth, not a tithe. Perhaps you will be no help after all. I am thinking of dismissing you."

"But, ma'am—"

The Priestess looked up, having been about to fall to some work.

"Ma'am, what can *you* tell me about these things? You have scattered only crumbs. I have extensive knowledge of incantation, poetry, magic, and I know these concern your problem. Give me what information you have, and I will be able to make use of mine in full. I am familiar with many sailors' tales. True, none of Aptor, or Hama, but I may be able to collate fragments. I have learned the legends and jargon of thieves through a broad life; this is more than your priests have, I'll wager. I have had teachers who were afraid to touch books I have opened. And I fear no secret you might know. If all of Leptar is in danger, you owe each citizen the right to try to save his brothers. I ask for that right alone."

"No, you are not afraid," admitted the Priestess. "You are honorable, and foolish . . . and a poet. I hope the first and last will wipe out the middle one in time. Nevertheless, I will tell you some." She stood up now, and drew out a map.

"Here is Leptar." She pointed to one island. Then her finger crossed water to another. "This is Aptor. Now you know as much about it as any ordinary person in Leptar might. It is a barbaric land, uncivilized. Yet they occasionally show some insidious organization. Tell me, what legends of the Great Fire have you heard?"

"I know that beasts are supposed to have come from the sea and destroyed the world's harbors, and that birds spat fire from the air."

"The older sailors," said the Priestess, "will tell you that these were beasts and birds of Aptor. Of course there are fifteen hundred years of retelling and distortion in a tradition never written down, and perhaps Aptor has simply become a synonym for everything evil, but these stories still give you some idea. Chronicles, which only three or four people have had access to, tell me that once, five hundred years ago, the forces of Aptor actually attempted to invade Leptar. The references to the invasion are vague. I do not know how far it went nor how successful it was, but its methods were insidious and very unlike any invasion you may have read of in history . . . so unlike, that records of it were destroyed, and no mention of it is made in the histories given to schoolchildren.

"Only recently have I had chance to learn how strange and inhuman they were. And I have good reason to believe that the forces of Aptor are congealing once more, a sluggish but huge amoeba of horror. Once fully awake, once launched, it will be unstoppable. Tendrils have reached into us for the past few years, probed, and then withdrawn before they were recognized. Sometimes they dealt catastrophic blows to the center of Leptar's government and religion. All this has been assiduously kept from the people. For if it were made known, we would also have to reveal how staggering is our ignorance, and there would be a national paralysis. I have been sent to clear perhaps just one more veil from the unknown. And if you can help me in that, you are welcome more than I could possibly express."

"What of the jewels, and of Hama?" inquired Geo. "Is he a god of Aptor under whom these forces are being marshaled? And are these jewels sacred to him in some way?"

"Both are true, and both are not true enough," replied the Priestess.

"And one more thing. You say the last attempted invasion by Aptor into Leptar was five hundred years ago. It was five hundred years ago that the religion of Argo in Leptar purged all her rituals and instituted new ones. Was there some connection between the invasion and the purge?"

"I am sure of it," declared the Priestess. "But I do not know what it is. However, let me now tell you the story of the jewels. The one I wear at my neck was captured, somehow, from Aptor during that first invasion. That we captured it may well be the reason that we are still a free nation today. Since then it has been guarded carefully in the Temple of the Goddess Argo, its secrets well protected, along with those few chronicles which mention the invasion—which ended, incidentally, only a month before the purges. Then, about a year ago, a small horde of horror reached our shore from Aptor. I cannot describe it. I did not see any of what transpired. But they made their way inland, and managed to kidnap Argo herself."

"You mean Argo Incarnate? The highest priestess?"

"Yes. Each generation, as you know, the first daughter of the past generation's highest priestess is chosen as the living incarnation of the White Goddess Argo. She is reared and taught by the wisest priests and priestesses. She is given every luxury, every bit of devotion; and she is made Argo Incarnate, until she marries and has daughters. And so it is passed on. At any rate, she was kidnapped. One of the assailants was hacked down: instantly it decayed, rotted on the floor of the convent corridor. But from the putrescent mass of flesh, we salvaged a second jewel from Aptor. And before it died, it was heard to utter the lines I quoted to you before. So, I have been sent then, to find what I can of the enemy, and to rescue or to find the fate of our young Argo."

"I will do whatever I can," said Geo, "to help save Leptar and to discover the whereabouts of your sister priestess."

"Not my sister," said the woman softly, "my daughter in blood, as I am the daughter of the last Argo: that is why this task fell to me. And until she is found dead, or returned alive"—there she rose from her bench—"I am again the White Goddess Argo Incarnate."

Geo dropped his eyes as Argo lifted her veil. Once more that evening she held forth the jewel. "There are three of these," she said. "Hama's sign is a black disk with three white eyes. Each eye represents a jewel. With the first invasion, they probably carried all three jewels, for the jewels are the center of their power. Without them, they would have been turned back immediately. With them, they thought themselves invincible. But we captured one, and very soon unlocked its secrets. I have no guards with me. With this jewel I need none. I am as safe as I would be with an army, and capable of nearly as much destruction.

"When they came to kidnap my daughter a year ago, I am convinced they carried both of their remaining jewels, thinking that we had either lost, or did not know, the power of the first. Anyway, they reasoned, they had two to our one. But now, we have two, and they are left with only one. Through some complete carelessness, your little thief stole one from me as I was about to board when we first departed two months ago. Today he probably recognized me and intended to exact some fee for its return. But now, he will be put to a true thief's task. He must steal for me the third and final jewel from Hama. Then we shall have Aptor, and be rid of their evil."

"And where is this third jewel?" asked Geo.

"Perhaps," said the woman, "perhaps it is lodged in the forehead of the statue of the Dark God Hama that sits in the guarded palace somewhere in the center of the jungles of Aptor. Do you think your thief will find himself challenged?"

"I think so," answered Geo.

"Somewhere in that same palace is my daughter, or her remains. You are to find them, and if she is alive, bring her back with you."

"And what of the jewels?" asked Geo. "When will you show us their power so that we may use them to penetrate the palace of Hama?"

"I will show you their power," said Argo, smiling. With one hand she held up the map over which she had spoken. With the other she tapped the white jewel with her pale fingernail. The map suddenly blackened at one edge, flared. Argo walked to a brazier and deposited the flaming paper. Then she turned once more to Geo. "I can fog the brain of a single person, as I did with Snake; or I can bewilder a hundred men. As easily as I can fire a dried, worn map, I can raze a city."

"With those to help," smiled Geo, "I think we have a fair chance to reach this Hama, and return."

But the smile with which she answered his was strange,

and then it was gone. "Do you think," she said, "that I would put such temptation in your hands? You might be captured, and if so, then the jewels would be in the hands of Aptor once more."

"But with them we would be so powerful—"

"They have been captured once; we cannot take the chance that they be captured again. *If* you can reach the palace, *if* you can steal the third jewel, *if* my daughter is alive, and *if* you can rescue her, then she will know how to employ its power to manipulate your escape. However, if you and your friends do not accomplish *all* these things, the trip will be useless; and so perhaps death would be better than a return to watch the wrath of Argo in her dying struggle, for you would feel it more horribly than even the most malicious torture of Aptor's evil."

Geo did not speak.

"Why do you look so strangely?" asked Argo. "You have your poetry, your spells, your scholarship. Don't you believe in their power? Go back to your berth. Send the thief to me." The last words were a sharp order, and Geo turned from the room into the dark. The sudden chill cleared the inside of his nostrils, and he stopped to look back at the door, then out to sea. A moment later he was hurrying to the forecastle.

CHAPTER THREE

~~~~~~

Geo walked down into the bunk room, still deserted except for Urson and Snake.

"Well?" asked Urson, sitting up on the edge of his berth. "What did she tell you?"

"Why aren't you asleep?" Geo said heavily. He touched Snake on the shoulder. "She wants to see you now."

Snake stood up, started for the door, then turned back.

"What is it?" Geo asked.

Snake dug into his clout again and pulled out the thong with the jewel. He walked over to Geo, hesitated, then placed the thong around the poet's neck.

"You want me to keep it for you?" Geo asked.

But Snake turned and was gone.

"Well," said Urson. "So you have one for yourself, now. I wonder what they do. Or did you find out? Come on, Geo, give up what she told you."

"Did Snake say anything to you while I was out?"

"Not a peep," answered Urson. "And I came no nearer sleep than I came to the moon. Now come on, what's this about?"

Geo told him.

When he finished, Urson said, "You're crazy. You and her. You're both crazy."

"I don't think so," Geo said. He concluded his story by recounting Argo's demonstration of the jewel's power.

Urson fingered the stone up from Geo's chest and looked at it. "All that in this little thing. Tell me, do you think you can figure out how it works?"

"I don't know if I want to," Geo said. "It doesn't sound right."

"Damn straight it doesn't sound right," Urson reiterated. "What's the point of sending us in there with no protection to do something that would be crazy with a whole army? What's she got against *us*?"

"I don't think she has anything against us," Geo said. "Urson, what stories do you know about Aptor? She said you might be able to tell me something."

"I know that no one trades with it, everyone curses by it, and the rest is a lot of rubbish not worth saying."

"Such as?"

"Believe me, it's just bilge water," insisted Urson. "Do you think you could figure out that little stone there, if you had long enough, I mean? She said that the priests five hundred years ago could, and she seems to think you're as smart as some of them. I wouldn't doubt you could work it."

"You tell me some stories first," said Geo.

"They talk about cannibals, women who drink blood, things neither man nor animal, and cities inhabited only by death. I'm fairly sure it's not what you'd call a friendly place, the way sailors avoid it, save to curse by; still, most of what they say is silly."

"Do you know anything more than that?"

"There's nothing more to know." Urson shrugged. "Every human ill there is at one time or another has been said to come from Aptor, whether it's the monsters that brought the Great Fire, or dandruff. I've never been there and I've never wanted to go. But I'll welcome the chance to see it so that on my next trip I can stop some of the stupid babble that's always springing up about it."

"She said the stories you'd tell would not be one tenth of the truth."

"She must have meant that there wasn't even a tenth part of the truth in them. And I'm sure she's right. You just misunderstood."

"I heard her correctly," Geo assured him.

"Then I just don't believe it. There are half a dozen things that don't match up in all this. First, how that little four armed fellow happened to be at the pier after two months just when she was coming in. And to have the jewel still, not have traded it, or sold it already—"

"Maybe," suggested Geo, "he read her mind too, when he first stole it, the same way he read ours."

"And if he did, maybe he knows how to work the things. I say let's find out when he comes back. And I wonder who cut his tongue out. Strange One or not, that makes me sick," grunted the big man.

"About that," Geo started. "Don't you remember? He said you knew the man it was."

"I know many men," said Urson, "but which one of the many I know is it?"

"You really don't know?" Geo asked, quietly.

"You say that in a strange way," Urson said, frowning.

"I'll say the same thing he said," went on Geo. "What man did you kill?"

Urson looked at his hands a while, stretched the fingers, turned them over in his lap like meat he was examining. Then, without looking up, he said: "It was a long time ago, friend, but the closeness of it shivers in my eyes. I should have told you, yes. But it comes to me, sometimes, not like a memory, but something I can feel, as hard as metal, taste it as sharp as salt, and the wind brings back my voice, his words, so clearly I shake like a mirror where the figure on the inside pounds his fists on the fists of the man outside, each one trying to break free.

"We were reefing sails in a flesh-blistering rain, when it began. His name was Cat. The two of us were the two biggest men aboard, and that we had been put on the reefing team together meant this was an important job to be done right. Water washed our eyes; our hands slipped on wet ropes. It was no wonder my cloth suddenly flung from me in a gust, billowing down in the rain, flapping against a half dozen ropes and breaking two small stays. 'You clumsy bastard,' bawled the Mate from the deck. 'What sort of fish fingered son of a bitch are you?'

"And through the rain I heard Cat laugh from his own spar. 'That's the way luck goes,' he cried, catching at his own cloth that threatened to pull loose. I pulled mine in and bound her tight. The competition that should go rightly between two fine sailors drove a seed of fury into my flesh that should have bloomed as a curse or a return jibe, but the rain rained too hard, and the wind rang too strong; so I bound my sail in silence.

"I was last down, of course; and as I was coming—there were men on deck—I saw why my sail had come loose. A worn mast-ring had broken and caused a main rope to fly and my canvas to come tumbling. But the ring also had held the nearly split aft mast together, and in the wind, a crack twice the length of my arm pulled open and snapped to, again and again, like a child's noise clapper. There was a rope near: inch thick line coiled on a spike. Holding myself to a rat-line mostly by my toes, I secured the rope and bound the base of the broken pole. Each time it snapped to, I looped it once around and pulled the wet line tight. They call this 'whipping' a mast, and I whipped it till the collar of rope was three feet long to the top of the cleft and she couldn't snap anymore. Then I hung the broken ring on a peg nearby so I could point it out to the ship's smith and get him to replace the rope with metal bands.

"That evening at mess, with the day's incidents out of my mind and hot soup in my mouth, I was laughing over some sailor's tale about another sailor and another sailor's woman, when the Mate strode into the hall. 'Hey, you sea scoundrels,' he bellowed. There was silence. 'Which of you bound up that broken mast aft?'

"I was about to call out, 'Aye, it was me' when another man beat me by bawling, 'It was the Big Sailor, sir!' That was a name both Cat and me were often hailed by.

" 'Well,' snarled the Mate, 'the Captain says that such good thinking in times hard as these should be rewarded.' He took a gold coin from his pocket and tossed it on the table in front of Cat. 'There you go, Big Sailor. But I think it's as much as any man should do.' And then he clomped from the mess hall. A cheer went up for Cat as he pocketed the coin; I couldn't see his face.

"The anger in me started now, but without direction. Should it go to the sailor who'd called out the name of the hero? Naw, for he had been down on deck, and through rain and darkness probably he could not have told me from my rival, anyway, at that distance. At Cat? But he was already getting up to leave the table. And the First Mate, the same

First Mate of this ship, friend, that we're on now, he was out stomping somewhere on deck.

"Perhaps it was this that caused my anger to break out the next morning when we were in calmer weather. A careless salt jarred me in a passageway, and suddenly I was all fists and fire. We scuffled, pounded one another, we cursed, we rolled: we rolled right under the feet of the Mate, who was coming down the steps at the time. He sent a boot into us and a lot of curses, and when he recognized me, he sneered, 'Oh, the clumsy one.'

"Now I'd had a fiery record before. Fights on ship are a breach few captains will allow. This was my third, and one too many. And the Mate, prompted by his own opinion of me, got the Captain to order me flogged.

"So, like meat to be sliced and bid on, I was led out before the assembled sailors at the next sunrise and bound to the mast. I thought my wrath went all toward the First Mate now. But black turned white in my head, hard as something to bite into, when he flung the whip to Cat and cried, 'Here, Big sailor, you've done your ship one good turn. Now rub sleep off your face and do it another. I want ten stripes on that one's back deep enough to count easily with a finger dipped in salt.'

"They fell, and I didn't breathe the whole time. Ten lashes is a whipping a man can recover from in a week. Most go down to their knees with the first one, if the rope is slack enough. I didn't fall until they finally cut the ropes from my wrists. Nor was it till I heard a second gold coin rattle down on the deck from the First Mate's hand and the words to the crew, 'See how a good sailor gets rich,' that I made a sound. And it was lost in the cheer which sprang from the other men.

"Cat and one other lugged me to the brig. As I fell forward, hands scudding into straw, I heard Cat's voice: 'Well, brother, that's the way luck goes.'

"Then the pain made me faint.

"A day later, when I could pull myself up to the window-bars and look out on the back deck, we caught the worst storm I'd ever seen. The slices in my back made it no easier on me. Pegs threatened to pull from their holes, boards to part themselves; one wave washed four men overboard, and while others ran to save them, another came and swept off six more. The storm had come so suddenly not a sail had been rolled, and now the remaining men were swarming to the rat-lines.

"From my place at the brig's window I saw the mast start to go and I howled like an animal, tried to pull the bars away. But legs passed my window running, and none stopped. I screamed at them, and I screamed again. The ship's smith had not yet gotten to fix my makeshift repair on the aft mast with metal. Nor had I yet even pointed it out to him as I had intended. It didn't hold ten minutes. When it gave there was a snap like thunder. Under the tug of half furled sails ropes popped like thread. Men were whipped off like drops of water shaken from a wet hand. The mast raked across the sky like a claw, and then fell against the high mizzen, snapping more ropes and scraping men from their perches as you'd scrape ants from a tree. The crew's number was halved, and when somehow we crawled from under the sheets of rain, one mast fallen and one more ruined, the broken bodies with still some life numbered eleven. A ship's infirmary holds ten, and the overflow goes to the brig. The choice of who became my mate was between the man most likely to live—he might take the harder situation more easily than the others—and the man most likely to die—it would probably make no difference to someone that far gone. The choice was made, the latter choice; and the next morning they carried Cat in and laid him beside me on the straw while I slept. His spine had been crushed at the pelvis and a spar had pierced his side with a long hole big enough to put your hand into.

"When he came to, all he did was cry—not with the agonized howls I had given the day before when I watched the mast topple, but with a little sound that escaped from clenched teeth, like a child who doesn't want to show the pain. It didn't stop. For hours. And such a soft sound, it burned into my gut and my tongue deeper than any animal wailing.

"The next dawn stretched copper foil across the window, and red light fell on the straw and the filthy blanket they had laid him in. The crying had been replaced now by gasps, sharp every few seconds, irregular, and so loud. I thought he must be unconscious, but when I kneeled to look, his eyes were opened and he stared into my face. 'You . . .' he hawked at me. 'It hurts. . . . You . . .'

" 'Be still,' I said. 'Here, be still!'

"The next word I thought I heard was 'water,' but there wasn't any in the cell. I should have realized that the ship's supplies had probably gone for the most part overboard. But by now, hungry and thirsty myself, I could see it as nothing less than a stupendous joke when one slice of bread and a tin cup of water were finally brought and with embarrassed silence handed in to us at seven that morning.

"Nevertheless, I opened his mouth and tried to pour some of it down his throat. They say a man's lips and tongue turn black from fever and thirst after a while. It's not true. The color is the deep purple of rotten meat. And every taste bud was tipped with that white stuff that gets in your mouth when your bowels stick for a couple of days. He couldn't swallow the water. It just dribbled over the side of his mouth that was scabby with crust.

"He blinked, and once more got out, 'You . . . you please . . .' Then he began to cry again.

" 'What is it?' I asked.

"Suddenly he began to struggle and got his hand into the breast of his torn shirt and pulled out a fist. He held it out toward me and said, 'Please . . . please . . .'

"The fingers opened and I saw three gold coins, two of whose histories suddenly returned to my mind like the stories of living men.

"I moved back as if burned; then I leaned forward again. 'What do you want?' I asked.

" ' . . . Please . . .' he said, moving his hand toward me. '. . . Kill . . . kill . . . me,' and then he was crying once more. 'It hurts so bad. . . .'

"I got up. I walked across to the other side of the cell. I came back. Then I broke his neck across my knee.

"I took up my pay. Later I ate the bread and drank the rest of the water. Then I went to sleep. They took him away without question. And two days later when the next food came, I realized, absently, that without the bread and water I would have starved to death. They finally let me out because they needed my muscle, what was left of it. And the only thing I sometimes think about, the only thing I let myself think about, is whether or not I earned my pay. I guess two of them were mine anyway. But sometimes I take them out and

look at them; and wonder where he got the third one from."
Urson put his hand in his shirt and brought out three gold
coins. "Never been able to spend them, though," he said. He
tossed the pile into the air, and then whipped them from their
arc into his fist again. He laughed. "Never was able to spend
them, on anything."

"I'm sorry," Geo said after a moment.

Urson looked up. "Why? I guess these are my jewels,
yes? Maybe everyone has theirs someplace. You think it was
old Cat, sometime when I was in the brig, perhaps, earning
that third coin, slicing out that little four armed bastard's
tongue? Somehow I doubt it."

"Look, I said I was sorry, Urson."

"I know," Urson said. "I know. I guess I've met a hell
full of people in my wet windy life; but it could be any one of
them." He sighed. "Though I wish I knew who. Still, I don't
think that's the answer." He lifted his hand to his mouth and
gnawed at his little fingernail. "I hope that kid doesn't get as
nervous as I do." He laughed. "He'll have such a hell of a lot
of nails to bite."

Then their skulls split.

"Hey," said Geo, "that's Snake!"

"And he's in trouble too!" Urson leaped to the floor and
started up the passageway. Geo came after him.

"Let me go first!" Geo said, "I know where he is."

They reached the deck, raced beside the cabins.

"Move," ordered Urson. Then he heaved himself against
the door: it flew open.

Inside, behind her desk, Argo whirled, her hand on her
jewel. "What is the—"

But the moment her concentration turned, Snake, who
had been immobile against the opposite wall, vaulted across
the bench toward Geo. Geo grabbed the boy to steady him,
and immediately one of Snake's hands was at Geo's chest
where the jewel hung.

"You fools! . . ." hissed Argo. "Don't you understand?
He's a spy for Aptor!"

There was silence.

Argo said: "Close the door."

Urson closed it. Snake still held Geo and the jewel.

"Well," she said. "It is too late now."

"What do you mean?" asked Geo.

"That had you not come blundering in, one more of Aptor's spies would have yielded up his secrets and then been reduced to ashes." She breathed deeply. "But he has his jewel now, and I have mine. Well, little thief, here's a statemate. The forces are balanced now." She looked at Geo. "How do you think he came so easily by the jewel? How do you think he knew when I would be at the shore? Oh, he's clever indeed, with all the intelligence of Aptor working behind him. He probably even had you planted without your knowing it to interrupt us at just that time."

"No, he—" began Urson.

"—We were walking by your door," Geo interrupted, "when we heard a noise and thought there might be trouble."

"Your concern may have cost us all our lives."

"If he's a spy, I gather that means he knows how this thing works," said Geo. "Let Urson and me take him—"

"Take him anywhere you wish!" hissed Argo. "Get out!"

Then the door opened. "I heard a sound, Priestess Argo, and I thought you might be in danger." It was the First Mate.

The Goddess Incarnate breathed deeply. "I am in no danger," she said evenly. "Will you please leave me alone, all of you."

"What's the Snake doing here?" Jordde suddenly asked, seeing Geo and the boy.

"I said, leave me!"

Geo turned, away from Jordde, and stepped past him onto the deck, and Urson followed him. Ten steps further on, he glanced back, and seeing that Jordde had emerged from the cabin and was walking in the other direction, he set Snake down on his feet. "All right, Little One. March!"

Once in the passage to the forecastle, Urson asked, "Hey, what's going on?"

"Well, for one thing, our little friend here is no spy."

"How do you know?" asked Urson.

"Because she doesn't know he can read minds."

"How do you mean?" Urson asked.

"I was beginning to think something was wrong when I came back from talking to the Priestess. You were too, and it lay in the same vein you were talking about. Why would our task be completely useless unless we accomplished all parts of her mission? Wouldn't there be some value in just returning her daughter, the rightful head of Leptar, to her former position? And I'm sure her daughter may well have collected some useful information that could be used against Aptor, so that would be some value even if we didn't find the jewel. It doesn't sound too maternal to me to forsake the young priestess if there's no jewel in it for mother. And her tone, the way she refers to the Jewel as *hers*. There's an old saying, from before the Great Fire even: 'Power corrupts, and absolute power corrupts absolutely.' And I think she has not a little of the un-goddess-like desire for power first, peace afterwards.''

"But that doesn't mean this one here isn't a spy for Aptor,'' said Urson.

"Wait a minute. I'm getting there. You see, I thought he was, too. The idea occurred to me first when I was talking to the Priestess and she mentioned that there were spies from Aptor. The coincidence of his appearance, that he had even managed to steal the jewel in the first place, that he would present it to her the way he did: all this hinted something so strange, that spy was the first thing I thought of, and she thought so as well. But she did not know that Snake could read minds and broadcast mentally. Don't you see? Ignorance of his telepathy removes the one other possible explanation of the coincidence. Urson, why did he leave the jewel with us before he went to see her?''

"Because he thought she was going to try and take it away from him.''

"Exactly. When she told me to send him to her, I was fairly sure that was the reason she wanted him. But if he was a spy, and knew how to work the jewel, then why not take it with him, present himself to Argo with the jewel, showing himself as an equal force; and then come calmly back, leaving her in silence and us still on his side, especially since he would be revealing to her something of which she was nine-tenths aware already, and she would watch him no more carefully than if it were unconfirmed.''

"All right,'' said Urson, "why not?''

"Because he was *not* a spy, and didn't know how to work the jewel. Yes, he had felt its power once. Perhaps he was going to pretend he had it hidden on his person. But he did not want her to get her hands on it for reasons that were strong, but not selfish. Here, Snake,'' said Geo. ''You know how to work the jewel now; don't you? But you learned from Argo just now.''

The boy nodded.

''Here, then. Why don't you take it?'' Geo lifted the jewel from his neck and held it out to him.

Snake drew back and shook his head violently.

''As I thought.''

Urson looked puzzled.

''Snake has seen into human minds, Urson. He's seen things directly that the rest of us only learn from a sort of secondhand observation. He knows that the power of this little bead is more dangerous to the mind of the person who wields it than it is to the cities it may destroy.''

''Well,'' said Urson, ''as long as she thinks he's a spy, at least we'll have one of them little beads and someone who knows how to use it. . . . I mean if we have to.''

''I don't think she thinks he's a spy anymore, Urson.''

''Huh?''

''I give her credit for being able to reason at least as well as I can. Once she found out he had no jewel on him, she knew that he was as innocent as you and I. But her only thought was to get it any way she could. When we came in, just when she was going to put Snake under the jewel's control, guilt made her leap backwards to her first and seemingly logical accusation for our benefit. Evil likes to cloak itself as good.''

They stepped down into the forecastle. By now a handful of sailors had come into the room. Most were drunk and snoring on berths around the walls. One had wrapped himself completely up in a blanket in the middle berth of the tier that Urson had chosen for Snake. ''Well,'' said Urson, ''it looks like you'll have to move.''

Snake scrambled to the top bunk.

''Now, look, that one was mine!''

Snake motioned him up.

''Huh? Two of us in one of those?'' demanded Urson. ''Look, if you want someone to keep warm against, go down and sleep with Geo there. It's more room and you won't get squashed against the wall. I'm a thrasher, and I snore.''

Snake didn't move.

"Maybe you better do what he says," Geo said. "I have an idea that—"

"You've got another idea now?" asked Urson. "Damn it. I'm too tired to argue." He stretched out, and Snake's slight body was completely hidden. "Hey, get your elbows out of there," Geo heard Urson mutter before there was only the gentle thundering of his breath. . . .

—mist suffused the deck and wet lines glowed phosphorescent silver; the sky was pale as ice, yet pricks of stars still dotted the bowl. The sea, once green, had bleached to blowing whiteness. The door of the windowless cabin opened and white veils flung forward from the form of Argo, who emerged like silver from the ash-colored door. The whole movement of the scene seemed to happen in the rippling of gauze under breeze. A dark spot, like a burn on a photograph negative, at her throat pulsed like a heart, like a black flame. She walked to the railing, peered over. In the white washing a skeletal hand appeared. It raised on a beckoning arm, and then fell forward in the water. Another arm raised now, a few feet away, beckoning, gesturing. Then three at once; then two more.

A voice as pale as the vision spoke: I am coming. I am coming. We sail in an hour. The Mate has been ordered to put the ship out before dawn. You must tell me now, creatures of the water. You must tell me.

Two glowing arms raised now, and then a blurred face. Chest high in the water, the figure listed backwards and sank.

Are you of Aptor or Leptar? *demanded the apparitional figure of Argo again in the thinned voice.* Are your allegiances to Argo or Hama? I have followed thus far. You must tell me before I follow further.

There was a whirling of sound which seemed to be the wind attempting to say: The sea . . . the sea . . . the sea . . .

But Argo did not hear, for she turned away and walked from the rail, back to her cabin.

Now the scene moved, turned toward the door of the forecastle. It opened, moved through the hall, more like birch and sycamore bark than stained oak, and went on. In the forecastle, the oil lamp seemed rather a flaring of magnesium.

The movement stopped in front of a tier of three berths; on the bottom one lay—Geo! But Geo with a starved, pallid face. His mop of hair was bleached white. On his chest was a pulsing darkness, a flame, a heart, shimmering with the indistinctness of absolute black. On the top bunk a great form like a bloated corpse lay. Urson! One huge arm hung over the bunk, flabbed, puffy, with no hint of strength.

In the center berth was an anonymous bundle of blankets completely covering the figure inside. On this the scene fixed, drew closer; and the paleness suddenly faded into shadow, into nothing. . . .

Geo sat up and knuckled his eyes.

The dark was relieved by lamp glow. Looking from under the berth above, he saw the gaunt Mate standing across the room. "Hey, you," Jordde was saying to a man in one of the bunks, "up and out. We're sailing."

The figure roused itself from the tangle of bedding.

The Mate moved to another. "Up, you dog face! Up, you fish fodder! We're sailing." Turning around, he saw Geo watching him. "And what's wrong with you?" he demanded. "We're sailing, didn't you hear? Naw, you go back to sleep. Your turn will come, but we need experienced ones now." He grinned briefly, and then went to one more. "Eh, you stink like an old wine cask! Raise yourself out of your fumes! We're sailing!"

CHAPTER FOUR

"That dream . . ." Geo said to Urson a moment after the Mate left. Urson looked down from his bunk.

"You had it too?"

Both turned to Snake.

"I guess that was your doing, eh?" Urson said.

Snake scrambled down from the upper berth.

"Did you go wandering around the deck last night and do some spying?" Geo asked.

By now most of the other sailors had risen, and one suddenly stepped between Urson and Geo. " 'Scuse me, mate," he said and shook the figure in the second berth. "Hey, Whitey, come on. You can't be that soused from last night. Get up or you'll miss the mess." The young Negro sailor shook the figure again. "Hey, Whitey . . ." The figure in the blankets was unresponsive. The sailor gave him one more good shake, and as he rolled over, the blanket fell away from the blond head. The eyes were wide and dull; the mouth hung open. "Hey, Whitey!" the black sailor said again. Then slowly, he stepped back.

Mist enveloped the ship three hours out from port. Urson was called for duty right after breakfast, but no one bothered either Snake or Geo that first morning. Snake slipped off somewhere and Geo was left to wander the ship alone. He was walking beneath the dories when the heavy slap of bare feet on the wet deck materialized into Urson.

"Hey," grinned the giant. "What are you doing under here?"

"Nothing much," Geo said.

Urson was carrying a coil of rope about his shoulder.

Now he slung it down into his hand, leaned against the support shaft, and looked out into the fog. "It's a bad beginning this trip has had. What few sailors I've talked to don't like it at all."

"Urson," asked Geo, "have you any ideas on what actually happened this morning?"

"Maybe I have and maybe I haven't," Urson said. "What ones have you?"

"Do you remember the dream?"

Urson scrunched his shoulders as if suddenly cold. "I do."

"It was like we were seeing through somebody else's eyes, almost."

"Our little four armed friend sees things in a strange way if that's the case."

"Urson, that wasn't Snake's eyes we saw through. I asked him, just before he went off exploring the ship. It was somebody else. All he did was get the pictures and relay them into our minds. And what was the last thing you saw?"

"As a matter of fact," Urson said, turning, "I think he was looking at poor Whitey's bunk."

"And who was supposed to be sleeping in poor Whitey's bunk?"

"Snake?"

"Exactly. Do you think perhaps Whitey was killed instead of Snake?"

"Could be, I guess. But how, and why, and who?"

"Somebody who wanted Snake killed. Maybe the same person who cut his tongue out a year and a half ago."

"I thought we decided that we didn't know who that was."

"A man you know, Urson," Geo said. "What man on this ship have you sailed with before?"

"Don't you think I've been looking?" Urson asked. "There's not a familiar face on deck, other than maybe one I've seen in a dockside bar, but never one whose name I've known."

"Think, Urson; who on this ship you've sailed with before," Geo asked again, more intently.

"Jordde!" Suddenly Urson turned. "You mean the Mate?"

"That's just who I mean," said Geo.

"And you think he tried to kill Snake? Why didn't Snake tell us?"

"Because he thought if we knew, we'd get in trouble with it. And he may be right."

"How come?" asked Urson.

"Look, we know something is fishy about Argo. The more I think about it, the less I can put my hands on it. But if something is fishy about the Mate too, then perhaps he's in cahoots with her. What about when he came into Argo's cabin last night when we were there?"

"Maybe he was just doing what we said we had been: walking by when he heard a noise. If it was his eyes we were seeing through, then he sees things awfully funny."

"Maybe he's a Strange One too, like Snake, who 'hears' things funny. Not all strangeness shows," Geo reminded him.

"You could be right. You could be right." He stood up from the lifeboat support. "Well, I've got something to do and I can't stand here all day. You think some more, friend, and I'll be willing to listen. I'll see you later." He hauled up his rope again and started off in the mist.

Geo looked around him, and decided to search for Snake. A ladder led to the upper deck; climbing it, he saw across the boards a tall, fog-shrouded figure. He paused, and then started forward. "Hello," he said.

The Captain turned from the railing.

"Good morning, sir," Geo said. "I thought you might be the Mate."

The Captain was silent for a while, and then said, "Good morning. What do you want?"

"I didn't mean to disturb you if you were—"

"No disturbance."

"How long will it take us to get to Aptor?"

"Another two weeks and a half. Shorter if this wind keeps up."

"I see," said Geo. "Have you any idea of the geography of Aptor?"

"The Mate is the only one on board who has ever set foot on Aptor and come off it alive. Except Priestess Argo."

"The Mate, sir? When?"

"On a previous voyage he was wrecked there. But he

made a raft and drifted into the open sea where he had the good fortune to be picked up in a ship.''

"Then he will lead whatever party goes to the place?"

"Not him," said the Captain. "He's sworn never to set foot on the place again. Don't even ask him to talk about it. Imagine what sort of a place it must be if probable death on the water is better than struggling on its land. No, he'll pilot us through the bay to the river's estuary, but other than that, he will have nothing to do with the place.

"Two other men we had on board who'd been there and returned. They went with the Priestess Argo in a boat of thirteen. Ten were dismembered and the pieces of their bodies were thrown in the water. Two survived to row the Priestess back to the boat. One was the sailor called Whitey, who died in the forecastle this morning. Not half an hour ago, I received news that the other one went overboard from the rigging and was lost in the sea. This is not a good trip. Men are not to be lost like coins in a game. Life is too valuable.''

"I see," said Geo. "Thank you for your information and time, sir.''

"You are welcome," the Captain said. Then he turned away.

Geo descended the ladder and walked slowly along the deck. Something touched him on the shoulder; he whirled.

"Snake, God damn it, don't do that!''

The boy looked embarrassed.

"I didn't mean to yell," Geo said, putting his hand on the boy's shoulder. "Come on, though. What did you find? I'll trade you what I know for what you do.''

you . . . sleep . . . came from Snake.

"I'm sorry, friend," laughed Geo. "But I couldn't take a nap now for money. You're just going to have to 'yell' yourself hoarse and answer some fairly direct questions. And whether knowing the answer is going to get me in trouble or not, you answer right. First of all, whose eyes were we seeing through last night? The Captain's?"

Snake shook his head.

"The Mate's?''

Snake nodded.

"Thought so. Now, did he want to kill . . . wait a minute," said Geo. "Can the Mate read minds too? Is that why you're keeping things from us?"

Snake shrugged.

"Come on now," Geo said. "Do a little yelling and explain."

don't . . . know . . . Snake thought out loud. *can . . . see . . . what . . . he . . . sees . . . hear . . . what . . . he . . . hears . . . but . . . no . . . hear . . . thoughts . . .*

"I see. Look, take a chance that he can't read minds and tell me. Did he kill the man in the bed you should have been in?"

Snake paused for a minute. Then nodded.

"Do you think he was trying to kill you?"

Snake nodded again.

"Now, one other thing. Did you know that the man who was killed this morning in your place was one of the two men who came back from Aptor with the Priestess Argo on her last expedition?"

Snake looked surprised.

"And that the other one drowned this morning, fell overboard, and was lost?"

Snake jumped.

"What is it?"

look . . . for . . . him . . . all . . . morning . . . he . . . not . . . dead . . . hear . . . thoughts . . . dim . . . low . . .

"Who's not dead?" Geo asked. "Which one?"

second . . . man

"Did you find him?" Geo asked.

can't . . . find . . . Snake said, *but . . . alive . . . I . . . know . . .*

"One other question." Geo lifted the jewel from against his chest. "How do you work this silly thing?"

think . . . through . . . it . . . said Snake.

Geo frowned. "What do you mean? Can you tell me how it works?"

you . . . have . . . no . . . words . . . Snake said. *radio . . . electricity . . . diode . . .*

"Radio, electricity, diode?" repeated Geo, the sounds coming unfamiliarly to his tongue. "What are they?"

Snake shrugged.

Thirty feet in front of them the door to Argo's cabin opened, and the veiled Priestess stepped out. She saw them;

at once her hand raised to her throat. Then it dropped. Snake and Geo were still.

Above, on the deck that topped the cabins, the dim form of the Mate was distinguishable; but Geo could not tell whether Jordde was watching them or had his back to them.

The Priestess paused, and then returned to her room.

And the Mate walked away from the rail.

Geo got a chance to report his findings to Urson that evening. The big sailor was puzzled.

"Can't you add anything?" Geo asked.

"All I've had a chance to do is work," grumbled Urson. They were standing by the rail beyond which the mist steeped thickly, making sky and water indistinguishable and grave. "Hey, Four Arms," Urson asked suddenly, "what are you looking at?"

Snake stared at the water but said nothing.

"Maybe he's listening to something," suggested Geo.

"You'd think there were better things to eavesdrop on than fishes," said Urson. "I guess Argo's given special orders that you two get no work. Some people. Let's go eat." As they started toward the convergence of sailors at the entrance of the mess hall, Urson paused. "Oh, guess what." He picked up the jewel from Geo's chest. "All you people are going around with such finery, I took my coins to the smithy and had him put chains on them. Now I'll strut with the best of you." He laughed as they went through the narrow way, crowding with the other sailors into the wide hall.

Night without dreams left them early; and the boat rolled from beneath the fog. Dawn was gray, but clear; by breakfast-time a ragged slip of land hemmed the horizon. Halfway through the meal, water was splashing from the brims of pitchers to roll one way, darkening the wooden table; then as the boat heaved it rolled another.

On the wheel-deck the sailors clustered at the rail. Before them rocks stuck like broken teeth from the water. Urson, in his new triple necklace, joined Snake and Geo.

"Whew! Getting through them is going to be fun."

Suddenly heads turned. The sailors looked back as Argo's dark veils, bloated with the breeze, filled about her as she mounted the steps to the wheel-deck. Slowly she walked among the sailors. They moved away. She stopped, one hand on a stay-rope, to stare across the water at the dark tongue of land.

From the wheel the Captain spoke: "Jordde, disperse the men and take the wheel."

"Aye, sir," said the Mate. "You, you, and you to the tops." He pointed among the men. "You also, and you. Hey, didn't you hear me?"

"Me, sir?" Geo turned.

"Yes, you; up to the top spar there."

"You can't send him up!" Urson called out. "He's never been topside at all before. It's too choppy for any lad's first time up. He doesn't even know—"

"And who asked you?" demanded the Mate.

"Nobody asked me, sir," said Urson, "but—"

"Then you get below before I brig you for insubordination and fine you your three gold baubles. You think I don't recognize dead man's gold?"

"Now look here!" Urson roared.

Geo looked from Argo to the Captain. The Captain was puzzled, true; but the bewilderment that flooded the face of the Priestess shocked him.

Jordde suddenly seized up a marlin pin, raised it, and shouted at Urson: "Get down below before I break your skull!"

Urson's fists sprang up.

"Calmly, brother bear—" Geo began.

"In a bitch's ass," snarled Urson and swung his arm forward. Something leaped on Jordde from behind—Snake! The belaying pin veered inches away from Urson's shoulder. The flung fist sank into the Mate's belly and he reeled forward with Snake still clawing at his back. He reached the rail, bent double over it, and Snake's legs flipped. When Jordde rose, he was free of encumbrance.

Geo rushed to the rail and saw Snake's head emerge in the churning water. Behind him, Urson yelled, "Look out!" Geo dodged aside as Jordde's spike made three inches of splinters in the plank against which he had been leaning.

"Not him!" cried Argo. "No, no! Not him!"

But Jordde seized Geo's shoulder and whirled him back against the rail. Geo saw Urson grab a hanging rope and swing forward. Urson tried to knock Jordde away with his feet. But Argo moved in the way of his flying body, and raised her hands to push him aside so that he swung wide and landed on the railing a yard from the struggle.

Then Geo's feet slipped on the wet boards; his body hurled backwards into the air. Then his back slapped water.

As he broke surface, Urson called to him. "Hang on, friend Geo, I'm coming!" Urson swung his arms back, then forward; he dove.

Now Geo could see only Argo and Jordde at the rail. But they were struggling!

Urson and Snake were near him in the water. The last thing he saw: Jordde suddenly wrested the chain from Argo's neck and flung it out into the sea. Her hands reached for the flying jewel, followed its arc as she screamed toward the water.

Then hands were at his body. Geo turned in the water as Snake disappeared beneath; Urson suddenly cried out. Hands caught Geo's arms as he tried to gulp a breath. And Urson was gone.

Hands were pulling him down.

Roughness of sand beneath one of his sides and the flare of sun on the other. His eyes were hot and his lids orange over them. Then there was a breeze. He opened his eyes, and shut them quick, because of the light. He turned over, thought about pillows and stiff new sheets. Reaching out, he grabbed sand.

He opened his eyes and pushed himself up. His hands spread on warm, soft crumblings. Over there were rocks, thick vegetation behind them. He swayed to his knees, the sand grating under his kneecaps. He looked at his arm in the sun, flecked with grains. Then he touched his chest.

His hand came to one bead, moved on, and came to another! He looked down. Both the chain with the platinum claw and the thong with the wire cage hung around his neck. Bewildered, he heaved to his feet. And sat down again as the beach went red with the wash of blood behind his eyeballs.

He got up again, slowly. The sand was only warm, which meant the clouds that had hung so thickly at dawn couldn't have been gone for long.

Carefully Geo started down the beach, looking toward the land. When he turned to look at the water, he stopped.

At the horizon, beyond the rocks, was the boat, with lowered sails. So they hadn't left yet. He swung his eyes back to the beach: fifty feet away was a man lying in the sun.

He ran forward, now, the sand splashing around his feet, sinking under his toes, so that it was like the slow motion running of dreams. Ten feet from the figure he stopped.

It was a young Negro, with skin the color of richly humused soil. The long skull was shaved. Like Geo, he was almost naked. There was a clot of seaweed at his wrist, and the soles of his feet and one upturned palm were grayish and shriveled; Geo thought about what happened when he sat in the bath too long.

He frowned and stood for a full minute. He looked up and down the beach once more. There was no one else. Just then the man's arm shifted across the sand like a sleeper's.

Immediately Geo fell to his knees beside the figure, rolled him over and lifted his head. The eyes opened, squinted in the light, and the man said, "Who are you?"

"My name is Geo."

The man sat up, and caught himself from falling forward by jamming his hands into the sand. He shook his head, then looked up again. "Yes," he said. "I remember you. What happened? Did we founder? Did the ship go down?"

"Remember me from where?" Geo asked.

"From the ship. You were on the ship, weren't you?"

"I was on the ship," Geo said. "And I got thrown overboard by that damned First Mate in a fight. But nothing's happened to the ship. It's still out there; you can see it." Suddenly Geo stopped. Then he said, "You're the guy who discovered Whitey's body that morning!"

"That's right." He shook his head again. "My name is Iimmi." Now he looked out to the horizon. "I see them," he said. "There's the ship. But where are we?"

"On the beach at Aptor."

Iimmi screwed his face up into a mask of dark horror.

"No . . ." he said softly. "We couldn't be. We were days away from . . ."

"How did you fall in?"

"It was blowing up a little," Iimmi explained. "I was in the rig when suddenly something struck me from behind and I went toppling. I thought a spar had come loose and knocked me over. In all the mist, I was sure they wouldn't see me, and the current was too strong for me, and . . ." He stopped, looked around.

"You've been on this beach once before, haven't you?" Geo asked.

"Once," said Iimmi. "Yes, once . . ."

"Do you realize how long you've been in the water?" Geo asked.

Iimmi looked up.

"Over two weeks!" Geo said. "Come on; see if you can walk. I've got a lot of things to explain, if I can, and we've got some hunting to do."

"Is there any water on this place?" Iimmi asked. "I feel like I could dry up and blow away." He got to his feet, swayed, straightened.

"Find water," said Geo. "A good idea. Maybe even a large river. And once we find it, I want to stay close to it as possible as long as I'm on this place, because we've got some friends around here."

Iimmi steadied himself, and they started up the beach.

"What are you looking around for?" Iimmi asked.

"Friends," Geo said.

Two hundred feet up, rocks and torpid vegetation cut off the beach. Scrambling over boulders and through vines, they emerged on a rock embankment that dropped fifteen feet into the wide estuary. A river wound back into the jungle. Twenty feet further, the bank dropped to the water's surface. They fell flat on wet rock and sucked in cool liquid, watching the blue stones and white and red pebbles shiver.

There was a sound. They sprang from the water and crouched on the rock.

"Hey," Urson said, through the leaves. "I was wondering when I'd find you." Light through branches lay more gold on the gold hung against his hairy chest. "Have you seen Snake?"

"I was hoping he was with you," said Geo. "Urson, this is Iimmi, the other sailor who died two weeks ago!"

Both Iimmi and Urson looked puzzled. "Have a drink of water," Geo said, "and I'll explain as best I can."

"Don't mind if I do," said Urson.

While the bear man lay down to drink, Geo began the story of Aptor and Leptar for Iimmi. When he finished, Iimmi asked, "You mean those fish things in the water carried us here? Whose side are they on?"

"Apparently Argo isn't sure either," Geo said. "Perhaps they're neutral."

"And the Mate?" asked Iimmi. "You think he pushed me overboard after he killed Whitey?"

"I thought you said he was trying to kill Snake," said Urson, who had finished drinking.

"He was," explained Geo. "He wanted to get rid of all three. Probably Snake first, and then Whitey and Iimmi. He wasn't counting on our fishy friends, though. I think it was just luck that it was Whitey he got rather than Snake. If he can't read minds, which I'm pretty sure he can't, he probably overheard you assigning the bunks for us to sleep in, Urson. When he found out he had killed Whitey instead, it just urged him to get Iimmi out of the way more quickly."

"Somebody tried to do me in," Iimmi agreed. "But I still don't see why."

"If there is a spy from Aptor on the ship, then Jordde is it," said Geo. "The Captain told me he had been to Aptor once before. It must have been then that he was enjoined into their forces. Iimmi, both you and Whitey had also been on Aptor's shore, if only for a few hours. There must be something that Jordde learned from the Island that he was afraid you might learn, something you might see. Something dangerous, dangerous for Aptor; something you might see just from being on the beach. Probably it was something you wouldn't even recognize; possibly you wouldn't see the significance of it until much later. But it probably was something very obvious."

Now Urson asked: "What did happen when you were on Aptor? How were those ten men killed?"

In the sun, Iimmi shivered. He waited a moment, then began: "We took a skiff out from the ship and managed to get through the rocks. It was evening when we started. The moon, I remember, had risen just above the horizon, though the sky was still blue. 'The light of the full moon is propitious to the White Goddess Argo,' she said from her place at the bow of the skiff. By the time we landed, the sky was black behind her, and the beach was all silvered, up and down. Whitey and I stayed to guard the skiff. As we sat on the gunwale, rubbing our arms against the slight chill, we watched the others go up the beach, five and five, with Argo behind them.

"Suddenly there was a scream. They came like vultures. The moon was overhead now, and a cloud of them darkened the white disk with their wings. They scurried after the fleeing men, over the sand. All we could really make out was a dark struggle on the silver sand. Swords raised in the white light, screams, and howls that sent us staggering back into the ocean. . . . Argo and a handful of those men left began to run toward the boat. They followed them down to the edge of the water, loping behind them, half flying, half running, hacking one after another down. I saw one man fall forward and his head roll from his body while blood shot ten feet along the sand, black under the moon. One actually caught at Argo's veils, but she screamed and slipped away into the water; she climbed back into the boat, panting. You would think a woman would collapse, but no. She stood in the bow while we rowed our arms off. They would not come over the water. Somehow we managed to get the skiff back to the ship without foundering against the rocks."

"Our aquatic friends may have had something to do with that," said Geo. "Iimmi, you say her veils were pulled off. Tell me, do you remember if she was wearing any jewelry?"

"She wasn't," Iimmi said. "She stood there in only her dark robe, her throat bare as ivory."

"She wasn't going to bring the jewel to Aptor where those monsters could get their hands on it again," said Urson. "But, Geo, if Jordde's the spy, why did he throw the jewel in the sea?"

"Whatever reason he had," said Geo, "our friends have given them both to me, now."

"You said Argo didn't know whose side these sea creatures were on, Leptar's or Aptor's," said Iimmi. "But perhaps Jordde knew, and that's why he threw it to them." He paused for a moment. "Friend, I think you have made an error; you tell me you are a poet, and it is a poet's error. The hinge in your argument that Snake is no spy is that Argo must have dubious motives to send you on such an impossible task, without protection, saying that it would be meaningful only if all its goals were accomplished. You reasoned, how could an honest woman place the life of her daughter below the value of a jewel—"

"Not just her daughter," interrupted Geo, "but *the* Goddess Argo Incarnate."

"Listen," said Iimmi. "Only if she wished to make permanent her temporary return to power, you thought, could she set such an impossible task. There may be some truth in what you say. But she herself would not bring the jewel to the shores of Aptor, though it was for her own protection. Now all three jewels are in Aptor, and, if any part of her story is true, Leptar right now is in more danger than it has been in five hundred years. You have the jewels, two of them, and you cannot use them. Where is your friend Snake who can? Both Snake and Jordde could easily be spies and the enmity between them feigned, so that while you were on guard against one, you could be misled by the other. You say he can project words and images into men's minds? Perhaps he clouded yours."

They sat silent for the lapsing of a minute.

"Argo may be torn by many things," continued Iimmi. "But you, in watching some, may have been deluded by others."

Light from the river quivered on the undersides of the leaves.

Urson spoke now. "I think his story is better than yours, Geo."

"Then what shall we do now?" asked Geo, softly.

"Do what the Goddess requests as best we can," said Iimmi. "Find the Temple of Hama, secure the stone, rescue the young Goddess, and die before we let the jewels fall into hands of Aptor."

"From the way you describe this place," muttered Urson, "that may not be far off."

"Still," mused Geo, "there are things that don't mesh.

Why were you saved too, Iimmi? Why were we brought here at all? And why did Jordde want to kill you and the other sailor?''

"Perhaps," said Iimmi, "the God Hama has a strange sense of humor and we shall be allowed to carry the jewels up to the temple door before we are slaughtered, dropping them at his feet." He smiled. "Then again, perhaps your story is the correct one, Geo, and I am the spy, sent to sway your reason."

Urson and Geo glanced at each other.

"There are an infinite number of theories for every set of facts," Geo said at last. "Rule number one: assume the simplest, that includes all the known conditions, to be true until more conditions arise for which the simplest theory no longer holds. Rule number two: then, and not until, assume another."

"Then we go into the jungle," Iimmi said.

"I guess we do," said Urson.

Geo stood up. "So far," he said, "the water creatures have saved us from death. Is there an objection to following the river island? It's as good a path as any, and it may mean more safety to us."

"No objection here," said Iimmi.

"What about the jewels?" asked Urson. "Perhaps we ought to bury them someplace where no one could ever find them. Perhaps if they were just completely out of the way . . ."

"It may be another 'poet's error,'" said Geo, "but I'd keep them with us. Even though we can't use them, we might be able to bluff our way with them."

"I'm for keeping them too," said Iimmi.

"Though I'm beginning to wonder how good any of my guesses are," Geo commented.

"Now don't be like that," cajoled Urson. "Since we've got this job, we've got to trust ourselves to do it right. Let's see if we can put one more of those things around your neck before we're through." He pointed to the two jewels hanging at Geo's chest. Then he laughed. "One more and you'll have as many as me." He rattled his own triple necklace.

CHAPTER FIVE

~~~~~~

Light lowered in the sky as they walked beside the river, keeping to the rocky bank and brushing away vines that strung into the water from hanging limbs. Urson broke down a branch thick as his wrist and tall as himself, and playfully smote the water. "That should put a bruise on anyone who wants to bother us." He raised the stick and drops ran the bark, sparks at the tips of dark lines.

"We'll have to go into the woods for food, soon," said Geo, "unless we wait for animals to come down to drink."

Urson tugged at another branch, and it twisted loose from fibrous white. "Here." He handed it to Geo. "I'll have one for you in a moment, Iimmi."

"And maybe we could explore a little, before it gets dark," Iimmi suggested.

Urson handed him the third staff. "There's not much here I want to see," he muttered.

"Well, we can't sleep on the bank. We've got to find a place hidden in the trees."

"Can't you see what's through there?" Geo asked.

"Where?" asked Iimmi. "Huh . . . ?" Through the thick growth was a rising shadow. "A rock or a cliff?"

"Maybe," mused Urson, "but it's awfully regular."

Geo started off into the underbrush; they followed. The goal was further and larger than it had looked from the bank. Once they crossed an area where large stones fit side by side, like paving. Small trees had pushed up between some of them, but for thirty feet, before the flags sank in the soft jungle, it was easier going. Then the forest thinned again and they reached a relatively clear area. Before them a ruined building loomed. Six girders cleared the highest wall. The

54

original height must have been eight or ten stories. One wall had completely sheared away and fragments of it chunked the ground. Broken rooms and severed halls suggested an injured granite hive. They approached slowly.

To one side a great metal cylinder lay askew a heap of rubbish. A flat blade of metal transversed it, one side twisting into the ground where skeletal girders showed beneath ripped plating. Windows like dark eyes lined the body, and a door gaped in an idiot oval halfway along its length.

Fascinated, they turned toward the injured wreck. As they neared, a sound came from inside the door. They stopped, and their staves leaped a protective inch from the ground. In the shadow of the door, ten feet above the ground, another shadow moved, resolving into an animal's muzzle, gray, long. They could see the forelegs. Like a dog, it was carrying a smaller beast, obviously dead, in its mouth. It saw them, watched them, was still.

"Dinner," Urson said softly. "Come on." They moved forward again. They they stopped.

The beast sprang from the doorway. Shadow and distance had made them completely underestimate its size. Along the sprung arc flowed a canine body nearly five feet long. Urson struck it from its flight with his stick. As it fell, Iimmi and Geo were upon it with theirs, clubbing its chest and head. For six blows it staggered and could not gain its feet. Then, as it threatened to heave to standing, Urson rushed forward and jabbed his stave straight down on the chest: bones snapped, tore through the brown pelt, their blue sheen covered a moment later by blood. It howled, kicked its hind feet at the stake with which Urson held it to the ground; then it extended its limbs and quivered. The front legs stretched, and stretched, while the torso pulled in on itself, shrinking in the death agonies. The long mouth, which had dropped its prey, gaped as the head flopped from side to side, the pink tongue lolling, shrinking.

"My God!" breathed Geo.

The sharp muzzle had blunted now and the claws in the padded paw stretched, opened into fingers and a thumb. The hairlessness of the underbelly had spread to the entire carcass. Hind legs lengthened, and bare knees bent as now human feet dragged through the brown leaves and a human thigh gave a

final contraction, stilled, and one leg fell out straight again.
The shaggy, black haired man lay on the ground, his chest
caved and bloody. In one last spasm, he flung his hands up
and grasped the stake to pull it from his chest; too weak, his
fingers slipped back down as his lips snarled open over his
perfectly white, blunt teeth.

Urson stepped back, then back again. The stave fell,
pulled loose with a sucking explosion from the ruined mess of
lung. The bear man had raised his hand to his own chest and
touched his triple, gold token. "In the name of the Goddess!" he finally whispered.

Geo walked forward now, picked up the carcass of the
smaller animal that had been dropped, and turned away.
"Well," he said, "I guess dinner isn't going to be as big as
we thought."

"I guess not," Iimmi said.

They walked back to the ruined building, away from the
corpse.

"Hey, Urson," Geo said at last. The big man was still
holding his coins. "Snap out of it. What's the matter?"

"The only man I've ever seen whose body was broken
in that way," he said slowly, "was one whose side was struck
in a ship's spar."

They decided to settle that evening at the corner of one
of the building's ruined walls. They made fire with a rock
against a section of rusted girder. After much sawing on a
jagged metal blade protruding from a pile of rubble, they
managed to quarter the animal and rip most of the pelt from
its red body. With thin branches to hold the meat, they did a
passable job of roasting. Although it was partially burned,
partially raw, and without seasoning, they ate it, and hunger
stopped. As they sat at the fire by the wall, ripping red juicy
fibers from the bones, night swelled through the jungle,
imprisoning them in the shell of orange flicker.

"Shall we leave it going?" asked Urson. "Fire keeps
animals away."

"If there are animals," reminded Geo, "and they do
want anything to eat . . . well, they've got that thing back
there."

On leaves raked together they stretched out by the wall.

There was quiet, no insect hum, no unnameable chitterings, except the comforting river rush beyond the trees.

Geo woke first, eyes filled with silver. He was dreaming again the strange happenings he had dreamed before. . . . No. He sat up: the entire clearing had flooded with white light from the amazingly huge disk of the moon sitting on the rim of the trees. The orange of the fire had comfortably bleached before it. Iimmi and Urson looked uncomfortably corpse-like. He was about to reach over and touch Iimmi's outstretched arm when there was a noise behind him. Beaten cloth? He jerked his head around, and was staring at the gray wall. He looked up the concrete that tore off raggedly against the night. There was nothing but stone and jagged darkness. Fatigue had snarled into something unpleasant and hard in his belly that had little to do with tiredness. He stretched his arm in the leaves once more and put his cheek down on the cool flesh of his shoulder.

The beating came again, continued for a few seconds. He rolled his face up and stared at the sky. Something crossed on the moon. The beating sounded once more. He raised his eyes further. Something . . . no, several things were perched on the broken ledge of the wall. A shadow shifted there; something waddled along a few feet. Wings spread, drew in again.

The flesh on his neck, his back, his chest, grew cold, then began to tickle. He reached out, his arm making thunder in the leaves, and grabbed Iimmi's black shoulder. Iimmi grunted, started, rolled over on his back, opened his eyes—Geo saw the black chest drop with expelled breath. A few seconds later the chest rose again. Iimmi turned his face to Geo, who raised his finger to his lips. Then he turned his face back up to the night. Three more times the flapping sounded behind them, behind the wall, Geo realized. Once he glanced down again and saw that Iimmi had raised his arm and put it over his eyes.

They spent a few years that way. . . .

A flock suddenly leaped from the wall, fell toward them, only to catch air in a billow of wings across the moon. They circled, returned to the wall, and then, after a pause, took off again. Some of them fell twenty feet before the sails of their wings filled and they began to rise again. They circled wider this time, and before they returned, another flock dropped down on the night.

Then Geo grabbed Iimmi's arm and pulled it down from his eyes. The shapes dropped like foundering kites: sixty feet above them, forty feet, thirty. There was a piercing shriek. Geo was up on his feet, and Iimmi beside him, their staffs in hand. The shadows fell, shrieking; wings began to flap violently, and they rose again, moving out from the wall. Now they turned back.

"Here it comes," whispered Geo. He kicked at Urson, but the big sailor was already on his knees, then feet. The wings beat, insistent and dark before them, flew toward them, then at the terrifying distance of five feet, reversed. "I don't think they can get in at the wall," Geo mouthed.

"I hope the hell they can't," Urson said.

Twenty feet away they hit the ground, black wings crumpling in the moonlight. In the growing horde of shadow, light snagged on a metal blade.

Two of the creatures detached themselves from the others and hurled themselves forward, swords arching suddenly above their heads in silver light.

Urson grabbed Geo's staff and swung it as hard as he could, catching both beasts on the chest. They fell backwards in an explosion of rubbery wings, as though they had stumbled into sheets of dark canvas.

Three more leaped the fallen ones, shrieking. As they came, Urson looked up and jammed his staff into the belly of a fourth about to fall on them above. One got past Iimmi's whistling staff and Geo grabbed a furry arm. He pulled it to the side, overbalancing the sailed creature. It dropped its sword as it lay for a moment, struggling on its back. Geo snatched the blade and brought it up from the ground into the gut of another who spread its wings and staggered back. He yanked the blade free, and turned it down into the body of the fallen one; it made a sound like a suddenly crushed sponge. The blade came out and he hacked into a shadow on his left. And a voice suddenly, but inside his head . . .

the . . . jewels . . .

"Snake!" bawled Geo. "Where the hell are you?" He still held his staff; now he flung it forward, spear-like, into the face of an advancing beast. Struck, it opened up like a black silk parachute, knocking back three of its companions before it fell.

His view cleared for an instant; Geo saw the boy, white under the moonlight, dart from the jungle edge. Geo ripped the jewels from his neck and flung the handful of chain and leather over the heads of the shrieking beasts. At the top of their arc the beads made a double eye in the light, before they fell on the leaves beyond the assailants. Snake ran for the jewels, picked them up, and held them above his head.

Fire leaped from the boy's hands in a double bolt that converged among the dark bodies. Red light cast a jagged wing in silhouette. A high shriek, a stench of burnt fur. Another bolt of fire fell in the dark horde. A wing flamed, waved flame about it. The beast tried to fly, but fell, splashing fire. Sparks sharp on a brown face chiseled it with shadow, caught the terrified red bead of an eye, and laid light along a pair of fangs.

Wings afire withered on the ground; dead leaves sparked now, and whips of flame ran in the clearing. The beasts retreated, and the three men stood against the wall, panting. Two last shadows suddenly dropped from the air toward Snake, who still stood with raised arms out in the clearing.

"Watch out!" Iimmi called to him.

Snake looked up as wings fell at him, tented him, hid him momentarily. Red flared beneath, and suddenly they fell away, sweeping the leaves—moved by wind or life, Geo couldn't tell. Wings rose on the moon, circled further away, were gone.

"Let's get out of here!" Urson said. They ran forward toward Snake.

Geo said: "Am I ever glad to see you!"

Urson looked up after the disappearing figures. "Let's get out of here."

Glancing back, they saw the fire had blown back against the wall and was dying. They walked quickly toward the forest. "Snake," said Geo when they stopped, "this is Iimmi. Iimmi . . . we told you about him."

Iimmi extended his hand. "Pleased to meet you."

"Look," said Geo, "he can read your mind, so if you still think he's a spy . . ."

Iimmi grinned. "Remember your general rule? If he is a

spy, it's going to get much too complicated trying to figure why he saved us."

Urson scratched his head. "If it's a choice between Snake and nothing, we better take Snake. Hey, Four Arms, I owe you a thrashing." He paused, then laughed. "I hope someday I get a chance to give it to you. Sometimes you seem more trouble than you're worth."

"Where have you been, anyway?" Geo asked. He put his hand on the boy's shoulder. "You're wet."

"Our water friends again?" suggested Urson.

"Probably," said Geo.

Snake now held one hand toward Geo.

"What's that? Oh, you don't want to keep them?"

Snake shook his head.

"All right," said Geo. He took the jewels and put them around his neck again.

"So that's what our treasure can do," said Iimmi.

"And much more than that," Geo told him. "Why don't you take one, Iimmi. Maybe we better not keep them all together."

Iimmi shrugged. "I suppose it's a lot of weight for one person. I'll carry one of them."

Geo took the chain with the platinum claw from his neck and hung it around Iimmi's. As they moved through the moon dapples, the jewel blinked like an eye in his black chest. Snake beckoned them to follow him. They only stopped to pick up swords from among the shriveled darkness. As they passed around the corner of the broken building, Geo looked for the corpse they had left there, but it was gone.

"Where are we going?" asked Urson.

Snake only motioned them on. They neared the broken cylinder and Snake scrambled up the rubble under the dark hole through which the man-wolf had leaped earlier that evening. They followed cautiously.

At the door, Snake lifted the jewel from Geo's neck, and held it aloft. It glowed, now; blue-green light seeped into the corners and crevices of the ruined entrance. Entering, they stood in a corridor lined with the metal frames of double seats from which ticking and upholstery had either rotted or been carried off by animals for nests. Shreds of cloth hung at the windows, most of which were broken. Twigs and rubbish

ittered the metal floor. They walked between the seats towards
a door at the far end. Effaced signs still hung on the walls,
Geo could just distinguish a few letters on one white enam-
eled, but chipped and badly rusted plaque:

N . . SM . . K . . . . G

"Do you know what language that is?" asked Iimmi.

"I can't make it out," said Geo.

The door at the end was ajar, and Snake opened it all the
way. Something scuttered through a cracked window. The
jewel's light showed two seats broken from their fixtures.
Vines covered the front window in which only a few splinters
of glass hung on the rim. Draped in rotten fabric, metal rings
about wrists and ankles, two skeletons with silver helmets
had fallen from the seats . . . perhaps five hundred years before. Snake pointed to a row of smashed glass disks in front
of the broken seats.

radio . . . they heard in their minds.

Now he reached down into the mess on the floor and
dislodged a chunk of rusted metal. *gun* . . . he said, showing
it to Geo.

The three men examined it. "What's it for?" asked
Urson.

Snake shrugged.

"Are there any electricities, or diodes around?" asked
Geo, remembering the words from before.

Snake shrugged again.

"Why did you want to show us all this?" Geo asked.

The boy only started back toward the door. When they
reached the oval entrance, about to climb down, Iimmi
pointed to the ruins of the building ahead of them. "Do you
know what that building was called?"

barracks . . . Snake said.

"I know that word," said Geo.

"So do I," said Iimmi. "It means a place where they
used to keep soldiers together. It's from one of the old
languages."

"That's right," said Geo. "From when they had armies."

"Is this where the armies of Aptor are hidden?" Urson
asked. "Those horrors we just got through?"

"In there?" asked Geo. The broken edges were graye
now, blunted under the failing moon. "Perhaps. It sounde
like they came from in there, at first."

"Where to now?" Urson asked Snake.

The boy only started back toward the door. When they fo
lowed him into the denser wood where pearls of light scattere
the tree trunks. They emerged at the broad ribbon of silver, th
river, broken by rocks.

"We were right the first time," Geo said. "We shoul
have stayed here."

Ripple and slosh and the hiss of leaves along the fore
edge—these accompanied them as they lay down on the drie
moss behind the larger rocks. Boughs, hung with moss an
vines, shaded moonlight from them. The weight of relief o
them, they dropped, like stones down a well, into the brigl
pool of sleep—

*—bright pool of silver growing and spreading and wrii
kling into the shapes of mast, the deck rail, the powder white se
beyond the ship. Down the deck another figure, gaun
skeletal, approached. The features, distorted by whitenes
and pulled to grotesquerie, were those of the Captain.*

Oh, Mate, the Captain said.

Silence, while Jordde gave an answer they couldn't hea.

*Yes, answered the Captain. I wonder what she wants
too. His voice was hollow, etoliated as a flower grown i
darkness. The Captain knocked now on Argo's cabin door.
opened, and they stepped in.*

*The hand that opened the door was thin as winter twig
The walls were draped in spider webs, hanging insubstanti
as layered dust. The papers on top of the desk were tissu
thin, threatening to scatter and crumble with a breath. Th
chandelier gave more languishing white smoke than ligh
and the arms, branches, and carved oil cups looked for a
the world like a convocation of spiders.*

Argo's pale voice sounded like thin webs tearing.

So, she said. We will stay at least another seven days.

But why? asked the Captain.

I have received a sign from the sea.

*I do not wish to question your authority, Priestess . . . beg
the Captain.*

Then do not, *interrupted Argo.*

My Mate has raised the objection that—

Your Mate has raised his hand to me once, *stated the Priestess. It is only my benevolence—here she paused, and her voice became unsure—that I do not . . . destroy him where he stands. Beneath her veil, her face might have been a skull's.*

But—*began the Captain.*

We wait here by the island of Aptor another seven days, *commanded Argo. She looked away from the Captain now, straight into the eyes of the Mate. From behind the veil, hate welled from the black sockets.*

They turned to go. On deck, they stopped to watch the sea. Waves like gray smoke swirled away: beyond that, at the horizon, a sharp tongue of land licked dark mountains. The cliffs were chalky on one side, streaked with red and blue clays on the other. There was a reddish glow beyond one peak, like a shimmering volcano. Dark as most of it was, the black was backed with purple, or broken by the warm, differing grays of individual rocks. Even through the night, at this distance, beyond the silver crescent of the beach, the jungle looked rich, green even in the darkness, redolent, full, and quiveringly heavy with life—

Then the thin screams—

CHAPTER SIX

~~~~~~

Geo rolled over and out of sleep, stones and moss
nibbling his shoulder. He grabbed his sword and was on his
feet. Iimmi was also standing with raised blade. Dawn was
white and gray through the trees. The air was chill, and the
river slapped coldly behind them.

The thin scream came again, like a hot wire drawn down
the gelid morning. Snake and Urson were also up, now. The
sounds came from the direction of the ruined barracks. Geo
started forward, cautiously, curiosity pulling him toward the
sound, fear pushing him from the relatively unprotected bank
and into the woods. The others followed.

Abruptly they reached the forest's rim, beyond which
was the clear space before the broken building. They crouched
now, behind the trees, to watch, fascinated.

Between ape and man, it hovered in the shadow of the
wall. It was Snake's height, but Urson's build. An animal
pelt wrapped its middle and went over its shoulder, clothing it
more fully than any of the four humans observing. Thick
footed, great handed, it loped four steps across the clearing,
uttered its piercing shriek, and fell on one of the beasts that
had dropped from the sky last night, rolling its head back and
forth as it tore at the corpse. Once it raised its head and a
sliver of flesh shook from its teeth before it fell again to
devour.

Suddenly another rushed from the forest. Halfway across
the clearing, it stopped over a piece of fallen carnage ten feet
from Geo's hiding place. As it crouched before them, they
watched the huge fingers upon broad flat palms, tipped with
bronze claws, convulse again and again in the fibrous meat.
The tusked mouth ripped.

64

A third entered from the woods now, slowly. It was smaller than the others. Suddenly it sighted a slain body from the night's encounter. It paused, stooped, then fell on the throat with bared teeth. Whether it was a breeze, or a final reflex, Geo couldn't tell: one of the membranous sails raised darkly and beat about the oblivious thing that fed.

"Come on," Urson whispered. "Let's go."

A thin scream sounded, and they started.

The first figure crouched apishly before them, head to the side with deep, puzzled eyes blinking below the ridged brow. The clawed fingers opened and closed like breathing, and the shaggy head was knotted with dirt and twigs. The breath hissed from the faintly shifting, full lips.

Urson reached for his sword, but Geo saw him and whispered, "No, don't . . ." Geo extended his hand and moved slowly forward.

The hulking form took a step back, and mewed.

Iimmi suddenly caught the idea. Coming up beside Geo, he made a quick series of snaps with his fingers and said in a coaxing, baby voice: "Come, come come . . ."

Geo laughed softly to Urson back over his shoulder. "It won't hurt us."

"If we don't hurt it," added Iimmi. "It's some sort of necrophage."

"A what?" asked Urson.

"It only eats dead things," Geo explained. "They're mentioned in some of the old legends. Apparently, after the Great Fire, so the story goes, there were more of these things around than anything else. In Leptar, though, they became extinct."

"Come here, cutie," said Iimmi. "Nice little, sweet little, pretty little thing."

It mewed again, bowed its head, came over and rubbed against Iimmi's hip. "Smells like hell," the black sailor observed, scratching behind its ear. "Watch out there, big boy!" The beast gave a particularly affectionate rub that almost upset Iimmi's balance.

"Leave your pet alone," said Urson, "and let's get going."

Geo patted the simian skull. "So long, beautiful." They turned toward the river again.

*   *   *

As they emerged on the rocky bank, Geo said, "At least we know we have seven days to get to the Temple of Hama and back again."

"Huh?" asked Iimmi.

"Don't you remember the dream, back on the ship?"

"You had the same dream too?"

Geo put his arm around Snake's shoulder. "Our friend here can relay other people's thoughts to you while you sleep."

"Who was thinking that?" asked Iimmi.

"Jordde, the First Mate."

"He makes everybody look dead. I thought I was having a nightmare. I could hardly recognize the Captain."

"You see one reason for believing Jordde's a spy?"

"Because of the way he sees things?" Again Iimmi smiled. "A poet's reason, I'm afraid. But I see."

The thin shriek sounded behind them, and they turned to see the hulking form crouched on the rocks above them.

"Uh-oh," said Urson, "there's your cute friend."

"I hope we haven't picked up a tagalong for the rest of the trip," said Geo.

It loped down over the rocks and stopped just before them.

"What's it got?" Iimmi asked.

"I can't tell," said Geo.

Reaching into the bib of its pelt, it brought out a gray hunk of meat and held it toward them.

Iimmi laughed. "Breakfast," he said.

"That!" demanded Urson.

"Can you suggest anything better?" Geo asked. He took the meat from the beast's claws. "Thanks, gorgeous."

It turned, looked back, and bounded up the bank and into the forest again.

Geo turned the meat in his hands, examining it. "There's no blood in it at all," he said, puzzled. "It's completely drained."

"That just means it'll take longer to spoil," said Iimmi.

"I'm not eating any of that," Urson stated.

"Do you think it's all right to eat, Snake?" Geo asked. Snake shrugged, and then nodded.

"Are you eating any?"

Snake rubbed his belly and nodded again.

"That's enough for me," said Geo.

With fire from the jewels, and wooden spits from the forest, they soon had the meat crackling and brown. Grease bubbled down its sides and hissed onto the hot stones they had used to rim the flame. Urson sat apart, sniffed, and then moved closer, and finally plowed big fingers across his hairy belly and grunted, "Damn it, I'm hungry!" They made room for him at the fire.

Sun struck the tops of the trees for the first time that morning, and a moment later light splashed concentric curves on the water, the gold stain spreading further and further.

"I guess time's getting on," said Urson, tearing a greasy handful of meat. He ducked his head to lick the juice running down his wrist.

"Well," said Geo, "now we know we have two friends."

"Who?" asked Urson.

"Up there." Geo pointed back to where the ape-beast had disappeared in the forest. "And down there." He pointed to the river.

"I guess we do," said Urson.

"Which reminds me," Geo continued, turning to Snake. "Where the hell were you before you got here last night? Come on, now, a little mind yelling."

beach . . . said Snake.

"And our fishy friends got you up here by way of the river after us?"

Snake nodded.

"How come we didn't find you on the beach before when Urson and Iimmi and me got together?"

not . . . yet . . . get . . . there . . . Snake said.

"Then where were you?"

ship . . .

"You were back on the ship?"

not . . . on . . . ship . . . Snake said. Then he shook his head. *too . . . complicated . . . to . . . explain . . .*

"It can't be that complicated," said Geo. "Besides, even with all the help you've been, you're under some pretty heavy suspicion."

Suddenly Snake stood up and motioned them to follow. They rose and followed him, Urson still chewing a mouthful of meat. As they scrambled up the bank again, back into the woods, Urson asked, "Where are we going now?"

Snake merely beckoned them on, accompanied by a gesture to be silent. In a minute they were back in the clearing by the barracks. There was not a bone or body left. As they went, Geo glimpsed Urson's fallen stave, dark with blood on one end. It lay alone in the leaves. Snake led them to the base of the ruined barracks. The sun was high enough to put yellow edges on the grass blades blowing against the wall. Snake paused once more, lifted the jewel from Iimmi's neck, and made a light with it. A second time he cautioned silence, and then stepped over the broken threshold of the first empty cubicle.

They crossed the cracked cement floor to the black rectangle of another doorway. Snake stepped through. They followed. Just beyond the edge of the sunlight, in the artificial illumination from the jewel, huge, rumpled, black sacks hung close together along naked pipes of the exposed plumbing along the ceiling. They walked forward until they found one single sack more or less alone. Snake brought the light close to its bottom and waved it there.

"Is he trying to tell us they can't see?" whispered Urson.

They whirled on the big sailor with fingers against their lips. At the same time there was a rustling like wet paper from the sack as one wing defined itself, and in the uncovered, upside-down face, a blind red eye blinked . . . then closed. The wing folded, and they tiptoed back across the chamber and into the sunlight. No one spoke until they could see the river again.

"What were you—" began Geo; his voice sounded annoyingly loud. More softly he said, "What were you trying to tell us?"

Snake pointed to Urson.

"What he said? That they can't see, just hear."

Snake nodded.

"Gee, thanks," said Geo. "I figured *that* out last night."

Snake shrugged.

"That still doesn't answer his questions," said Iimmi.

"And another one," said Geo. "Why are you showing

us all these things? You seem to know your way around awfully well. Have you ever been on Aptor before?"

Snake paused for a moment. Then he nodded.

They were all silent.

Finally Iimmi asked, "What made you ask that?"

"Something in that first theory," Geo said. "I've been thinking it for some time. And I guess Snake here knew I was thinking it, too. Jordde wanted to get rid of Iimmi, Whitey, and Snake, and it was just an accident that he caught Whitey first instead of Snake. He wanted to get rid of Whitey and Iimmi because of something they'd seen, or might have seen, when they were on Aptor with Argo. I just thought perhaps he wanted to get rid of Snake for the same reason. Which meant he might have been on Aptor before."

said that's when he became a spy for them."

They all looked at Snake again.

"I don't think we ought to ask him any more questions," said Geo. "The answers aren't going to do us any good, and no matter what we find out, we've got a job to do, and seven, no . . . six and a half days to do it in."

"I think you're right," said Iimmi.

"You *are* more trouble than you're worth," Urson addressed the boy. "Get going."

Then Snake handed the metal chain with the pendant jewel back to Iimmi. The black youth hung it on his chest once more. They started up the river.

By twelve, the sun had parched the sky. They stopped to swim and cool themselves. Chill water gave before reaching arms and lowered faces. They even dove for their aquatic helpers, but grubbed the pebbly bottom of the river with blind fingers, coming up with dripping twigs and wet stones. Soon, they were in a splashing match, of which it is fair to say, Snake won—hands down.

Later they lay on the mossy rocks to dry, slapping at small bugs, the sun like gold coins, warm on their eyelids. "I'm hungry," said Urson, rolling over.

"We just ate," Iimmi said, sitting up. ". . . I'm hungry too."

"We ate five hours ago," Geo said. The sun curved

loops of liquid metal in the ripples. "And we can't lie around here all day. Do you think we can find one of those things we got from the . . . wolf, yesterday?"

"Or some nice friendly necrophage?" suggested Iimmi.

"Ugh." Urson shivered.

"Hey," Iimmi asked Geo, "does not asking Snake questions mean not asking him where the Temple is?"

Geo shrugged. "We'll either get there or we won't. If we were going wrong and he knew about it, he'd have told us by now if he wanted us to know."

"God damn all this running around in circles," Urson exclaimed. "Hey, you little four armed bastard, have you ever seen where we're going?"

Snake shook his head.

"Do you know how to get there?"

Snake shook his head.

"Fine!" Urson snapped his fingers. "Forward, maties; we're off for the unknown once more." He grinned, doubled his pace, and they started once more behind him.

A mile on, hunger again thrust its sharp finger into their abdomens. "Maybe we should have saved some of that stuff from breakfast," muttered Urson. "With no blood in it, you said it wouldn't have spoiled."

Geo suddenly broke away from the bank toward the forest. "Come on," he said. "Let's get some food."

The vines were even thicker here, and they had to hack through with swords. Where the dead vines had stiffened in the sun, it was easier going. The air had been hot at the river; here it was cool, damp, and wet leaves brushed their arms and shoulders. The ground gave spongily under them.

The building they came upon: tongues of moss licked twenty and fifty feet up the loosely mortared stones. A hundred yards from the water, the jungle came right to its base. The edifice had sunk a bit to one side in the boggy soil. It was a far more stolid and primitive structure than the barracks. They scraped and hacked to the entrance where two columns of stone, six feet at the base, rose fifty feet to support an arch. The stones were rough and unfinished.

"It's a temple!" Geo said suddenly.

The steps were strewn with rubbish, and what spots of

light spilled from the twisted jungle stopped at the total
shadow below the great arch. A line of blackness up one side
of the basalt door showed that it was ajar. Now they climbed
the steps, moving aside a fallen branch. Leaves chattered at
them. They kicked small stones from the cracks in the rock.
Geo, Iimmi, then Snake, and at last Urson, squeezed through
the door.

Ceiling blocks had fallen from the high vault so that
shafts of sun struck through the slow shift of dust to the
littered floor.

"Do you think it's Hama's Temple?" Urson asked. His
voice boomed in the stone room, magnified and hollow.

"I doubt it," whispered Geo. "At least not the one
we're supposed to find."

"Maybe it's an abandoned one," said Iimmi, "and we
can find out something useful from it."

Something large and dark flapped through a far shaft of
sun. With raised swords they stepped back. After a moment
of silence, Geo handed his jewel to Snake. "Make some light
in here. Quick."

The blue-green glow flowed from the upraised jewel in
Snake's hand. Columns supported the broken ceiling along
the sides of the temple. As the light flared, and flared
brighter, they saw that the flapping had come from a bird
perched harmlessly on an architrave between two columns. It
ducked its head at them, cawed harshly, then flew out one of
the apertures in the ceiling. The sound of its wings still
thrummed seconds after it had gone.

They could not see the altar, but there were doors
between the columns, and as their eyes grew sensitive, they
saw that one section of wall had not withstood time's sledge.
A great rent was nearly blocked with vines. A green shimmer
broke here and there through the foliage.

They started forward now, chips and pebbles rolling
before their toes, down the great chapel toward the altar.

Behind a twisted railing, and raised on steps of stone, sat
the ruins of a huge statue. Carved from black rock, a man sat
cross-legged on a dais. One arm and shoulder had broken off
and lay in pieces on the altar steps. The hand, fingers as thick
as Urson's thigh, lay just behind the altar rail. The idol's head

was missing. Both the hand still connected and the one on the steps looked as though they had once held something, but whatever it was had been removed.

Geo walked along the rail to where a set of stone boxes were placed like footstones along the side of the altar. "Here, Snake," he called. "Bring a light over here." Snake obeyed, and with Iimmi's and Urson's help, he loosened one of the lids.

"What's in there?" Urson asked.

"Books," said Geo, lifting out one dusty volume. Iimmi reached over his shoulder and with dark fingers turned the pages. "Old rituals," Geo said. "Look here." He stopped Iimmi's hand. "You can still read them."

"Let me see," Iimmi said. "I studied with Eadnu at the University of Olcse Olwn."

Geo looked up and laughed. "I thought some of your ideas sounded familiar. I was a pupil of Welis. Our teachers would never speak to each other! This is a surprise. So, you were at Olcse Ohwn too?"

"Um-hm," said Iimmi, turning pages again. "I signed aboard this ship as a summer job. If I'd known where we'd end up, I don't think I'd have gone, though."

Stomach pangs were forgotten momentarily, as the two looked at the rituals of Hama.

"They're not at all like those of the Goddess," Iimmi observed.

"Apparently not," agreed Geo. ". . . Wait!" Iimmi had been turning pages at random. "Look there!" Geo pointed.

"What is it?" Iimmi asked.

"The lines," Geo said. "The ones Argo recited. . . ." He read out aloud:

> *"Forked in the heart of the dark oak*
> *the circlet of his sash*
> *rimmed where the eye of Hama broke*
> *with fire, smoke and ash.*
>
> *Freeze the drop in the hand,*
> *break the earth with singing.*
> *Hail the height of a man,*
> *also the height of a woman.*

Take from the tip of the sea
salt and sea-kelp and gold,
fixed with a shaft in the brain
as the terror of time is old.

Salt on the walls of the heart.
Salt in each rut of the brain.
Sea-kelp ground in the earth,
Returning with gold again.

The eyes have imprisoned a vision.
The ash tree dribbles with blood.
Thrust from the gates of the prison
smear the yew tree with mud.

"It's the other version of the poem I found in the
prepurge rituals of Argo. I wonder if there were any more
poems in the old rituals of Leptar that parallel those of Aptor
and Hama?"

"Probably," Iimmi said. "Especially if the first invasion
from Aptor took place just before, and probably caused, the
purges."

"What about food?" Urson suddenly asked. He was
sitting on the altar steps. "You two scholars have the rest of
time to argue. But we may starve before you come to some
conclusion."

"He's right," said Iimmi. "Besides, we have to get
going."

"Would you two consider it an imposition to set your
minds to procuring us some food?" Urson asked.

"Wait a minute," Geo said. "Here's a section on the
burial of the dead. Yes, I thought so." He read out loud now:

"Sink the bright dead with misgiving
from the half-light of the living . . ."

"What does that mean?" asked Urson.

"It means that the dead are buried with all the
accouterments of the living. I was pretty sure of it, but I
wanted to check. That means that they put food in the
graves."

"First, where are we going to find any graves; and

second, I've had enough dead and half dead food." Urson stood up.

"Over here," cried Geo. With Snake following, they came to the row of sealed doors behind the columns along the wall. Geo looked at the inscription. "Tombs," he reported. He turned the handles, a double set of rings, which he twisted in opposite directions. "In an old, uncared-for temple like this, the lock mechanisms must have rusted by now if they're at all like the ancient tombs of Leptar."

"Have you studied the ancient tombs?" asked Iimmi excitedly. "Professor Eadnu always considered them a waste of time."

"That's all Welis ever talked about," laughed Geo. "Here, Urson; you set your back to this a moment."

Grumbling, Urson came forward, took the rings, and twisted. One snapped off in his hand. The other gave with a crumbling sound inside the door.

"I think that does it," Geo said.

They all helped pull now, and suddenly the door gave an inch, and then, on the next tug, swung free.

Snake preceded them into the stone cell.

On a rock table, lying on its side, was a bald, shriveled body. Tendons ridged the brown skin, along the arms, along the calves; bits of cloth still stuck here and there. On the floor stood sealed jars, heaps of parchment, piles of ornaments.

Geo moved among the jars. "This one has grain," he said. "Give me a hand." Iimmi helped him lug the big pottery vessel to the door.

Then a thin shriek scarred the dusty air, and both students stumbled. The jar hit the ground, split, and grain heaped over the floor. The shriek came again.

Geo saw, there on the broken wall across the temple, five of the ape-like figures crouched before the shingled leaves, silhouetted on the dappled green. One leaped down and ran, wailing, across the littered floor, straight for the tomb door. Two others followed, then two more. And more had mounted the broken ridge.

The loping forms burst into the cell, one, and then its two companions. Claws and teeth closed on the shriveled skin. Others screamed around the entrance. The body rolled beneath hands and mouths. One arm swept into the air above the lowered heads and humped backs. It fell on the edge of the rock table, broke at mid-forearm, and the skeletal hand fell to the floor, shattering.

They backed to the temple door, eyes fixed on the desecration. Then they turned and ran down the temple steps. Not till they reached the river, and the sunlight on the broad rocks touched them, did they still, or breathe deeply. They walked quietly. Hunger returned slowly after that, and occasionally one would look aside into the faces of the others in an attempt to identify the vanishing horror that still pulsed behind their eyes.

CHAPTER SEVEN

~~~~~~

A small animal crossed their path, and one of the Snake's hands scooped up a sharp rock and sunk it into the beast's head at an eye's blink. They quartered it on Iimmi's blade, and had almost enough to fill them from the roast made with fire from the jewels. Following their own shadows into the afternoon, they continued silently up the river.

It was Urson who first pointed it out. "Look at the far bank," he said.

The river had become slower, broader here. Across from them, even with the added width, they could make out a man-made embankment.

A few hundred meters further on, Iimmi sighted spires above the trees, still across the river. They could figure no explanations, till the trees ceased on the opposite bank and the buildings and towers of the great city broke the sky. Many of the towers were ruined or cracked. Nets of girders were silhouetted against the yellow clouds, where the skin of buildings had stripped away. Elevated highways looped tower after tower, many of them broken also, their ends dangling colossally to the streets. The docks of the city across the water were deserted.

It was Geo who suggested: "Perhaps Hama's Temple is in there. After all, Argo's largest temple is in Leptar's biggest city."

"And what city in Leptar is *that* big?" asked Urson, awfully.

"How do we get across?" asked Iimmi.

But Snake had already started down to the water.

"I guess we follow him," said Geo, climbing down the rocks.

Snake dove into the water. Iimmi, Geo, and Urson followed. Before he had taken two strokes, Geo felt familar hands grasp his body from below. This time he did not fight; there was a sudden sense of speed, of sinking through consciousness.

Then he was bobbing up in chill water. The stone embankment rose to one side and the broad river spread to the other. He shook dark hair from his eyes and sculled toward the stones. Snake and Urson bobbed at his right, and a second later, Iimmi, at his left. He switched from sculling into a crawl, wondering how to scale the stones, when he saw the rusted metal ladder leading into the water. He caught hold of the sides and pulled himself up.

The first rung broke with his full weight, dropping him half into the water again, and his hands scraped painfully along the rust. But he pulled himself up once more, planting his instep on the nub of the broken rung; it held. Reaching the top, he turned back to call instructions, "Keep your feet to the side." Snake came up now, then Urson. Another rung gave under the big man's bare foot when he was halfway up. As he sagged backwards, then caught himself, the rivets of the ladder tugged another inch out from the stone. But it held. Iimmi joined them on the broad ridge of concrete that walled the river. All together now on the wharf, they turned to the city.

Ruin stretched before them. The buildings on the waterfront looked as though they had been flung from the sky and broken on the street, rather than built there. Girders twisted through plaster, needling to rusted points.

They stepped down into the street and walked a narrow avenue between piles of debris from two taller buildings. After a few blocks the building walls were canyon height. "How are you going to go about looking for the Temple?" Urson asked.

"Maybe we can climb up and take a look from the top of one of these buildings," Geo suggested. They raised their eyes and saw that the sky was thick with yellow clouds. Where it broke, twilight seeped.

They turned toward a random building. A slab of metal had torn away from the wall. They stepped through, into a high, hollow room. Dim light came from white tubes about the wall. Only a quarter of them were lit; one was flickering. In the center of the room hung a metal sign:

NEW EDISON ELECTRIC COMPANY

Beneath it, in smaller letters:

"LIGHT DOWN THE AGES"

Great cylinders, four or five times the height of a man, humped over the floor under pipes, wires, and catwalks. The four made their way along one walk toward a spiral staircase that wound up to the next floor.

"Listen!" Urson suddenly said.

"What is it?" Geo asked.

One of the huge cylinders was buzzing.

"That one." Urson pointed. They listened, then continued. As they mounted the staircase, the great room turned about them, sinking. At last they stepped up into a dark corridor. A red light glowed at the end:

EXIT

Doors outlined themselves along the hall in the red haze. Geo picked one and opened it. Natural light fell on them. They entered a room with the outer wall torn away. The floor broke off irregularly over thrusting girders.

"What happened here?" Urson asked.

"See," Iimmi explained. "That highway must have crashed into the wall and knocked it away."

A twenty-foot ribbon of road veered into the room at an insane angle. The railing was twisted but the stalks of street lights were still intact along the edge.

"Do you think we could climb that?" asked Geo. "It doesn't look too steep."

"For what?" Urson wanted to know.

"To get someplace high enough to see if there's anything around that looks like a temple."

"Oh," said Urson in a reconciled voice.

As they started across the floor toward the highway, Geo suddenly called, "Run!" As they leaped onto the slanted sheet of concrete, a crack opened in the flooring over which they had just walked. Cement and tile broke away and crashed to the street, three stories down. The section of road on which they perched now wavered up and down a good three feet. As it came to rest, Geo breathed again and glanced down to the street. A cloud of plaster settled.

"That way is up," Urson reminded him, and they started. In general the walk was in good shape. Occasional sections of railing had twisted away, but the road itself mounted surely between the buildings on either side of them through advancing sunset.

It branched before them and they went left. It branched again, and again they avoided the right-hand road. A sign, half the length of a three masted ship, hung lopsidedly above them on a building to one side:

WMTH
THE HUB OF
WORLD NEWS,
    COMMUNICATION,
        & ENTERTAINMENT

As they rounded the corner of the building, Snake suddenly stopped and put his hand to his head.

"What is it?" asked Geo.

Snake took a step backwards. Then he pointed to WMTH. *it . . . hurts . . .*

"What hurts?" asked Geo.

Snake pointed to the building again.

"Is there someone in there thinking too loud?"

thinking . . . machine . . . Snake said. *radio . . .*

"A radio is a thinking machine and there's one in there that's hurting your head?" interpreted Geo, tentatively, and with a question mark.

Snake nodded.

" 'Yes' what?" asked Urson.

"Yes, there's a radio in there and it's hurting him," said Geo.

"How come the one he showed us before didn't hurt him?" Urson wanted to know.

Iimmi looked up at the imposing housing of WMTH. "Maybe this one's a lot bigger."

"Look," Geo said to Snake. "You stay here, and if we see anything, we'll come back and report, all right?"

"Maybe he can get through it," Urson said.

Snake looked up at WMTH, bit his lip, and suddenly started forward, resolutely. They watched him go, until after ten steps, he put his hands to his head and staggered backwards. Geo and Iimmi ran forward to help him. When they got back beyond the effects of WMTH, Snake's face looked drained and pale.

"You stay here," Geo said. "We'll be back. Don't worry.'"

"Maybe it stops later on," Urson said, "and if he ran forward, he could get out the other side. It may just stop after a hundred feet or so."

"Why so anxious?" asked Geo.

"The jewels," said Urson. "Who's going to get us out of trouble if we should meet up with anything else?"

They were silent then. Their shadows over the pavement faded as the yellow tinge of the sky fell before blue. "I guess it's up to Snake," Geo said. "Do you think you can make it?"

Snake paused, then shook his head.

Geo said to the others: "Come on."

A sudden click; lights flickered all along the edges of the road. Almost a third of the lights still worked and now flared along both sides of the rising ramp, closing with the distance through the twilight.

"Come on," Geo said again.

The lights wheeled double and triple shadows about them on the road as they reached the next turnoff that led to a still higher ramp. Geo looked back. Snake, miniature and dimmed by distance, sat on the railing, his feet on the lower rung, one pair of arms folded, one pair of elbows on his knees above a puddle of shadow.

"I hope someone is keeping track of where we're going," Geo said, a few hundred yards on.

"I can get us back to New Edison," said Iimmi. "If it'll do any good," he added.

"Just keep track of the turns," said Geo.

"I'm keeping," Iimmi assured him.

"By the time we get to the top of whatever we're trying to get to the top of," rumbled Urson, "we won't be able to see anything. It'll be too dark."

"Then let's hurry," Geo admonished.

Sunset smeared one side of the towers with copper while blue shadows slipped down the other. Smaller walkways led to the buildings around them. By way of a plastic covered stair, they mounted another eighty feet to a broader highway where they could look down on the necklace of light they had just left. New Edison and WMTH still towered behind them. There was an even taller building before them. They had cleared the lower roofs.

On this road fewer lights were working. There were often five or six dark in a row, so that they moved with only the glow of a neighboring roadway twenty yards to the side to light them. They were just about to enter another of these dark sections when a figure appeared in silhouette at the other end.

They stopped.

The figure was gone.

Deciding it was imagination, they started again, peering through the incomplete darkness on either side. A little further, Geo suddenly halted. "There . . ."

Two hundred feet ahead of them, what may have been a naked woman rose from the ground, and began to walk backwards until she disappeared into the next length of dark road.

"Do you think she was running away from us?" Iimmi asked.

Urson touched the jewel on Iimmi's chest. "I wish we had some more light around here."

"Yeah," Iimmi agreed. They continued.

The skeleton lay at the beginning of the next stretch of functioning lights. The rib cage marked sharp shadows on the pavement. The hands lay above its head, and one leg twisted over the other in an impossible angle.

"What the hell is that?" Urson asked. "And how did it get there?"

"It looks like it's been there a little while," said Iimmi.

"Do we turn back now?" Urson asked.

"A skeleton can't hurt you," Geo said.

"But what about the live one we saw?" countered
Urson.

". . . And here she comes now," Geo whispered.

In fact, two figures approached them. As Urson, Geo
and Iimmi moved closer, they stopped, one a few steps before
the other. Then they dropped. Geo couldn't tell if they fell, or
lay down quickly on the roadway.

"Go on?" asked Urson.

"Go on."

Pause.

"Go on," Geo repeated.

Two skeletons lay on the road where the figures had
disappeared a minute before. "They don't seem dangerous,"
Geo said. "But what do they do? Die every time they see us?"

"Hey," Iimmi said. "What's that? Listen."

It was a sickly, liquid sound, like mud dropping into
itself. Something was falling from the sky. No, not from the
sky, but from the roadway that crossed theirs fifty feet
overhead. Looking down again, they saw that a blob of
something was growing on the pavement ten feet from them.

"Come on," Geo said, and they skirted the mess dripping from the road above, and continued up the road. They
passed four more skeletons. The plopping behind them became a sloshing.

As they turned it emerged under the white and flaring
lamps. Translucent insides bubble-pocked and quivering, it
slipped forward, across the road, toward the skeletons. Impal-
ing itself on the bones, it flowed around them, covered them,
molded to them. A final surge, and its shapelessness contracted into arms, a head, legs. The naked man-thing pushed
itself to its knees and then stood, its flesh now opaque.
Eye sockets caved into the face. A mouth ripped low on the
skull, and the chest began to move. A wet, steamy sound
came from the mouth hole in irregular gasps.

It began to walk toward them, raising its hands from its
sides. Then, behind it in the darkness, they saw the others.

"Damn," said Urson. "What do they . . . ?"

"One, or both, of two things," Geo answered, backing
away. "More meat, or more bones."

"Whoops!" Iimmi said. "Back there!"

Behind them seven more stood, while the ones in front advanced. Urson slipped his sword from his belt. The gleam of the street light ran down the blade. Suddenly he lunged at the leading figure, hacked at an upraised arm, sprang back. Severed at the elbow, the wound dribbled down the figure's side.

The arm splashed on the macadam. Quivering, the gelatinous mud contracted from the bone. As Urson danced back, one of the figures behind the injured one stepped squarely on the blob, which attached itself to its ankle and was absorbed.

A covered flight of stairs had its entrance here, leading to the next level of highway. They ducked into it and fled up the steps. Geo glanced back once: one of the forms had reached the entrance and had started to climb. They were high enough to get some idea of the city. Outside the transparent covering of the steps, the city spread in a web of lights, rising, looping, descending like roller coaster tracks. Two glows caught him: beyond the river, a pale red haze flickered behind the jungle and was reflected on the water. The other was within the city, a pale orange, nested among the buildings.

He took all this in during a glance, as he ran up the steps. A gurgling became a roar behind them as they reached the top. Geo was only clear of the entrance when he yelled, "Run!"

They slipped from the doorway and staggered back. A mass of jelly the size of a two story house flopped against the entrance. They edged by its pulsing sides. The lamplight pierced its translucent sides, where a skull caught in the jelly swirled to the surface, then sank.

"By Argo . . ." swore Urson.

"Don't try to cut it again, Urson!" Geo said. "It'll drown us!"

It sucked from the entrance and shivered ponderously. Something was happening at the front. A half dozen figures were detaching themselves from the parent and preceding it.

Geo: "They can't go very fast—"

"Let's get the *hell* out of here!" Urson said.

They ran up the road, plunging suddenly into a darkened

section. There was a glow in front of them. Suddenly Urson yelled, "Watch it!"

Abruptly the road sheered away. They halted, and approached the edge slowly. The surface of the road tore away and the girders, unsupported, sagged toward the ruined stump of a building from which rose the orange glow. One wall of the building still stood, topped by a few girders that spiked the darkness. The glow came from the heart of the ruin.

"What do you think that is?" asked Geo.

"I don't know," said Iimmi.

It sloshed along the road behind them. They looked. In the shadow, numberless figures marched toward them. Suddenly the figures fell to the ground, and without a halt in the sound, flesh rolled from bone, congealed, and rose, quivering, into the light.

"Get going!" Geo ordered.

Iimmi started out first on the twisted beams that descended to the glowing pit.

"You're crazy," Urson said. It flopped another meter. "Hurry up," he added. With Urson in the middle, they started along the twenty inch width of girder. Lit from beneath, most of their bodies were in the shadow of the beam. Only their arms, outstretched for balance, burned with pale orange.

Before them, legible on the broken wall:

ATOMIC ENERGY FOR THE BETTERMENT
OF MAN

flanked by purple trefoils. The beams twisted sideways, and then dropped, to join others. Iimmi made the turn, dropped to his knees and hands, and then started to let himself down the four feet to the next small section of concrete. Once he saw something, let out a low whistle, but continued to lower himself to the straightened girder. Urson made the turn next. When he saw what Iimmi had seen, his hand shot to Geo's chest and grabbed the jewel.

Geo took his wrist. "That won't help us now," he said. "What is it?"

Urson expelled a breath, and then continued down, slowly, without speaking. Quickly Geo turned to drop—

The beam structure over which they had just come was

coated with trembling thicknesses of the stuff. Globs hung pendulously from the steel shafts, glowing in the light from below, quivering, smoking, dropping off into the darkness. Here and there something half human rose to look around, to pull the collective mass further on; but then it would fall back, dissolve. Sagging between the girders, noisome, thick, it bulged forward, burning in the pale light, smoking now, bits shriveling, falling away. Geo was about to go on. Then he called, "Wait a minute."

It wasn't making progress. It rolled to a certain point in the sherbert colored light, sagged, smoked, and dropped away. And smoked. And dropped.

"It can't get any further?" Urson asked.

"It doesn't look it," said Geo.

A skeleton stood, flesh running in the orange light. It tottered, steaming, and fell with a sucking noise, into hundreds of feet of shadow. Geo was holding tightly to the girder in front of him.

The orange light fell cleanly over his hand, wrist, shadow starting at his elbow.

What happened made him squeeze until sweat came: the gargantuan mass, which had only extended tentacles till now, pulsed to the jagged edge, and flung itself on the metal threads. It careened toward them. They jerked back.

Then it stopped.

It boiled, it burned, it writhed. And it sank, smoking, through the naked girder work. It tried to crawl back. Human figures leaped toward the road edge, missed, and plummeted like smoking bullets. It hurled a great pseudopod back toward the safety of the road; it fell short, flopped downward, and the whole mass shook. It slipped free of the beams, tentacles sliding across steel, whipping into air. Then it dropped, breaking into a dozen pieces before they lost sight of it.

Geo released the girder. "My arm hurts," he said.

They climbed back to the road. "What happened?" asked Iimmi.

"Whatever it was, I'm glad it did," said Urson.

Something clattered before them in the darkness.

"What was that?" asked Urson, stopping.

"My foot hit something," Geo said.

"What was it?" asked Urson.

"Never mind," said Geo. "Come on."

Fifteen minutes brought them to the stairway to the lower highway. Iimmi's memory proved good, and for an hour they went quickly, Iimmi making no hesitation at turnings.

"God," Geo said, rubbing his forearm. "I must have pulled hell out of my arm back there. It hurts like the devil."

Urson looked at his hands and rubbed them together.

"My hands feel sort of funny," Iimmi said. "Like they've been windburned."

"Windburned, nothing," said Geo. "This hurts."

Twenty minutes later, Iimmi said, "Well, this should be about it."

"Hey," said Urson. "There's Snake!" They ran forward as the boy jumped off the rail. Snake grabbed their shoulders, and grinned. Then he began to tug them forward.

"Lucky little so and so," said Urson. "I wish you'd been with us."

"He probably was, in spirit, if not in body," Geo laughed.

Snake nodded.

"What are you pulling for?" Urson asked. "Say, if you're going to get migraines at times like that, you'd better teach us what to do with them beads there." He pointed to the jewel at Iimmi's and Geo's necks.

But Snake just tugged them on.

"He wants us to hurry," Geo said. "We better get going."

The fallen floor had made descent through New Edison impossible. But the roadway still continued down, and so they followed it along. Twice it cracked widely and they had to clamber along the rail. All the street lights were out here, but they could see the river, struck with moonlight, through the buildings. Finally the road tore completely away, and four feet below them, over the twisted rail, was the mouth of the street that led to the waterfront. Snake, Iimmi, and then Urson vaulted over. Urson shook his hands painfully when he landed.

"Give me a hand, will you?" Geo asked. "My arm is really shot." Urson helped his friend over.

And almost as though it had been in wait, thick liquid gurgled behind them. A wounded thing, it emerged from behind the broken highway, bulging up into the light which shone on the wrinkles in its shriveled membrane.

"Run it!" bawled Urson. They took off down the street. In the moonlight, the ruined piers spread along the waterfront to either side.

They saw it bloat the entrance of the street, fill it, then pour across the broken flags, slipping across the rubble of the smashed buildings.

On the edge of the wharf they looked back. Now the thing wavered, spreading tentacles left and right. From one of these a man formed. Standing at the head of the flowing mess, he raised a hand and beckoned to them in the moonlight.

Geo hit water and was aware of two things immediately, as the hands caught him. First, the thong was yanked from around his neck. Second, pain seared his arm as if the nerves and ligaments were suddenly laced by white hot strands of steel. Every vein and capillary had become part of a web of fire.

It was a long time before consciousness. Once he was lifted, and he opened his mouth, expecting water. But there was only cool air. And when he opened his eyes, the white moon was moving fast above him toward the dark shapes of leaves, then was gone behind them. Was he being carried? And his arm . . . There was more drowsy half consciousness, and once a great deal of pain. When he opened his mouth to scream, however, darkness flowed in, swathed his tongue, and he swallowed the darkness down into his body and into his head, and called it sleep—

—*a spool of copper wire unrolled over the black tile. Scoop it up quick. Damn, let me get out of here. Run past the black columns, glimpsing the cavernous room, and the black statue at the other end, huge, rising into shadows. Men in dark robes walking around. Just don't feel up to praying this afternoon. I am before the door; above it, a black disk with three white eyes on it. Through the door, now, up the black stone steps. Wonder if anyone will be up there. Just my luck I'll find the Old Man himself. Another door with a black circle above it. Push it open slowly, cool on my hands. A man is standing inside, looking into a large screen. Figures*

*moving on it. Can't make them out; he's in the way. Oh,
there's another one. Jeepers . . .*

I don't know whether to call it success or failure, *one
says.*

The jewels are . . . safe or lost?

What do you call it? *the first one asks.* I don't know
anymore. *He sighs.* I don't think I've taken my eyes off
this thing for more than two hours since they got to the
beach. Every mile they've come has made my blood run
colder.

What do we report to Hama Incarnate?

It would be silly to say anything now. We don't know.

Well, *says the other,* at least we can do something with
the City of New Hope since they got rid of that super-
amoeba.

Are you sure they really got it?

After the burning it received over that naked Atom Pile?
It was all it could do to get to the waterfront. It's just about
fried up and blown away already.

And how safe would you call them? *the other asks.*

Right now? I wouldn't call them anything.

*Something glitters on the table by the door. Yes, there it
is. In the pile of junked equipment is a U-shaped scrap of
metal. Just what I need. Hot damn, adhesive tape too! Quick,
there, before they see. Fine. Now, let the door close, reeeeeal
slow. Oops. It clicked. Now come on; look innocent, in case
they come out. I hope the Old Man isn't watching. Guess
they're not coming. And down the stairs again; the black
stone walls moving past. Out another door, into the garden:
dark flowers, purple, deep red, some with blue in them, and
big stone urns. Oh, priests coming down the path. Oops
again, there's Dunderhead. He'll want me inside praying.
Duck down behind that urn. Here we go. What'll I do if he
catches me? Really sir, I have nothing under my choir robe.
Peek out.*

*Very, very small sigh of relief. Can't afford to be too loud
around here. They're gone. Let's examine the loot. The black
stone urn has one handle above. It's about eight feet tall.
One, two, three: jump, and . . . hold . . . on . . . and . . . pull.
And try to get to the top. . . . There we go. Cold stone between*

my toes. And over the edge, where it's filled with dirt. Pant. Pant. Pant.

Should be just over here, if I remember right. Dig, dig, dig. Damp earth feels good in your hands. Ow! my finger. There it is. A brown paper bag under the black earth. Lift it out. Is it all there? Open it up; peer in. At the bottom, in the folds of paper: tiny scraps of copper, a few long pieces of iron, a piece of board, some brads. To this my grubby little hand adds the spool of copper wire and the U-shaped scrap of metal. Now, slip it into my robe and . . . once you get up here, how the hell do you get down? I always forget. Turn around, climb over the edge, like this, and let yourself . . . Damn, my robe's caught on the handle.

And drop.

Skinned my shin again. Someday I'll learn. Uh-oh, Dunderhead is going to blow a condenser when he sees my robe torn. Oh well; sic vita est.

Now let's see if we can figure this thing out. Gotta crouch down and get to work. Here we go. Open the bag, and turn the contents out in the lap of my robe, grubby hands poking.

The U-shaped metal, the copper wire, fine. Hold the end of the wire to the metal, and maneuver the spool around the end of the rod. Around. And around. And around. Here we go round the mulberry-bush, the mulberry-bush, the mulberry-bush. Here we go round the mulberry-bush; I'll have me a coil by the morning.

A harsh voice: And what do you think you're doing?

Dunderhead rides again. Nothing, sir, as metal and scraps and wires fly frantically into the paper bag.

The voice: All novices under twenty must report to afternoon services without fail!

Yes, sir. Coming right along, sir. *Paper bag jammed equally frantically into the folds of my robe. Not a moment's peace. Not a moment's! Through the garden with lowered eyes, past dour priest with small paunch. There are mirrors along the vestibule, reflecting the blue and yellow from the colored panes. In the mirror I see pass: a dour priest, preceded by a smaller figure with short red hair and a spray of freckles over a flattish nose. As we pass into prayer, there is the maddening, not quite inaudible, jingle of metal, muffled by the dark robe—*

Geo woke up, and almost everything was white.

CHAPTER EIGHT

~~~~~~

The pale woman with the tiny eyes rose from over him. Her hair slipped like white silk threads over her shoulders. "You are awake?" she asked. "Do you understand me?"

"Am I at Hama's Temple?" he asked, the remnants of the dream still blowing in at the edges of his mind, like shredding cloth. "My friends . . . where are they . . . ?"

The woman laughed. "Your friends are all right. You came out the worst." Another laugh. "You ask if this is Hama's Temple? But you can see. You have eyes. Don't you recognize the color of the White Goddess Argo?"

Geo looked around the room. It was white marble, and there was no direct source of light. The walls simply glowed.

"My friends . . ." Geo said again.

"They are fine. We were able to completely restore their flesh to health. They must have exposed their hands to the direct beams of the radiation only a few seconds. But the whole first half of your arm must have lain in the rays for some minutes. You were not as lucky as they."

Another thought rushed Geo's mind now. *The jewels* . . . he wanted to say, but instead of sounding the words, he reached to his throat with both hands. One fell on his naked chest. And there was something very wrong with the other. He sat up in the bed quickly, and looked down. "My arm . . ." he said.

Swathed in white bandages, the limb ended some foot and a half short of where it should have.

"My arm . . . ?" he asked again, with a child's bewilderment. "What happened to my arm?"

"I tried to tell you," the woman said, softly. "We had

91

to amputate your forearm and most of your biceps. If we had not, you would have died.''

"My arm . . ." Geo said again. He lay back on the bed.

"It is difficult," the woman said. "It is only a little consolation, I know, but we are blind here. What burned your arm away, took our sight from us when it was much stronger, generations ago. We learned how to battle many of its effects, and had we not rescued you from the river, all of you would have died. You are men who know the religion of Argo, and adhere to it. Be thankful then that you have come under the wing of the Mother Goddess again. This is hostile country." She paused. "Do you wish to talk?"

Geo shook his head.

"I hear the sheets rustle." the woman said, smiling, "which means you either shook or nodded your head. I know from my study of the old customs that one means 'yes' and the other 'no.' But you must have patience with us who cannot see. We are not used to your people. Do you wish to talk?" she repeated.

"Oh," said Geo. "No. No, I don't."

"Very well." She rose, still smiling. "I will return later." She walked to a wall. A door slipped open, and then it closed behind her.

He lay still for a long time. Then he turned over on his stomach. Once he brought the stump under his chest and held the clean bandages in his other hand. Very quickly he let go, and stretched the limb sideways, as far as possible away from him. That didn't work either, so he moved it back down to his side, and let it lay by him under the white sheet.

After a long while, he got up, sat on the edge of the bed, and looked around the room. It was completely bare, with neither windows nor visible doors. He went to the spot through which she had exited, but could find no seam or crack. His tunic, he saw, had been washed, pressed, and laid at the foot of the bed. He slipped it over his head, fumbling with only one arm. Getting the belt together started out a problem, but he hooked the buckle around one finger and maneuvered the strap through with the others. He adjusted his leather purse, now empty, at his side.

His sword was gone.

An unreal feeling, white like the walls of the room,

filled him like a pale mixture of milk and water. He walked around the edge of the room once more, looking for some break.

There was a sound behind him and the tiny-eyed woman in her white robe stood in a triangular doorway. "You're dressed," she smiled. "Good. Are you too tired to come with me? You will eat and see your friends if you feel well enough. Or, I can have the food brought—"

"I'll come," Geo said.

He followed her into a hall of the same luminous substance. Her heels touched the back of her white robe with each step. His own bare feet on the cool stones seemed louder than those of the blind woman before him. Suddenly he was in a larger room, with benches. It was a chapel of Argo. But the altar at the far end, its detail was strange. Everything was arranged with the simplicity one would expect of a people to whom visual adornment meant nothing. He sat down on a bench.

"Wait here." She disappeared down another hall.

She returned, followed by Snake. Geo and the four armed boy looked at each other, silently, as the woman disappeared again. A wish, like a living thing, suddenly writhed into a knot in Geo's stomach, that the boy would say something. He himself could not.

Again she returned, this time with Urson. The big sailor stepped into the chapel, saw Geo, and exclaimed, "Friend ... what ..." He came to Geo quickly and placed his warm hands on Geo's shoulders. "How ..." he began, and shook his head.

Geo grinned suddenly, and patted his stump with his good hand. "I guess Jelly-belly got something from me, after all."

Urson took up Geo's good hand and examined it. It seemed pale. Urson held his own forearm next to Geo's and compared them. The paleness was in both. "I guess none of us got out completely all right. I woke up once while they were taking the scabs off. It was pretty bad, and I went to sleep again fast."

Iimmi came in now. "Well, I was wondering ..." He stopped, and let out a low whistle. "I guess it really got you, brother." His own arms looked as though they had been dipped in bleach up to the mid forearms, leaving them pinkish until they turned their normal purple-brown at the elbows.

"How did this happen?" Urson asked.

"When we were back doing our tightrope act on those damn girders," explained Iimmi, "our bodies were in the shadow of the girders and the rays only got to our arms. It's apparently a highly directional form of radiation, stopped by anything like steel, but . . ."

"A highly who of what?" Urson asked.

"I've been getting quite a course." Iimmi grinned. "And I've got something you'll be interested in, too, Geo."

"Just tell me where the hell we are," Urson said.

"We're in a convent sacred to Argo," Iimmi told him. "It's across the river from the City of New Hope, which is where we were."

"That name sounds familiar; in the—" began Urson. Snake gave him a quick glance; and Urson stopped, and then frowned.

"We knew of your presence in the City of New Hope," explained the blind Priestess, "and we found you by the riverside after you managed to swim across. We thought you would die, but you apparently have a stronger constitution than the inhabitants of Aptor. After crossing the river, you managed to cling to life long enough for us to get you back to the convent and apply what art we could to soothe the burns from the deadly fire."

There was no jewel around Iimmi's neck either. Geo could feel the hands ripping it from his neck in the water again. Iimmi must have just made the same discovery, when he looked at Geo, because his pale hand raised to his own chest.

"If you gentlemen will come with me," said the blind Priestess of Argo. "None of you have had more than intravenous feeding for the past two days. You may eat now." She turned down another hall; again they followed.

They arrived at an even larger room, this one set with white marble benches and long white tables. "This is the main dining room of the convent," their guide explained. "One table has been set up for you. You will not eat with the other priestesses, of course."

"Why not?" asked Iimmi.

Surprise flowed across the blind face. "You are men," she told them, matter-of-factly. Then she led them to a table with wine, meat, and bowls piled with strange fruit. As they sat, she disappeared once more.

Geo reached for a knife. For a moment there was silence as the nub of his arm jutted over the table. "I guess I just have to learn," he said after the pause. He picked up the knife with the other hand.

Halfway through the meal, Urson asked, "What about the jewels? Did the Priestess take them from you?"

"They came off in the water," said Iimmi.

Geo nodded corroboration.

"Well, now we really have a problem," said Urson. "Here we are, at a temple of Argo's, where we could return the jewels and maybe even get back to the Priestess on the ship and out of the silly mess, and the jewels are gone."

"That also means our river friends are working for Hama," said Geo.

"And we are just being used to carry the jewels back to Hama's Temple," added Urson. "Probably, when they found we were almost dead after that thing in the city, they just took the jewels from us and abandoned us on the shore."

"I guess so," said Iimmi.

"Well," Geo said, "Hama's got his jewels then, and we're out of the way. Perhaps he delivered us into Argo's hands as a reward for bringing them this far."

"Since we would have died anyway," said Iimmi, "I guess he was doing us a favor."

"And you know what that means," Geo said, looking at Snake now.

"Huh?" asked Urson. Then he said, "Oh, let the boy speak for himself. All right, Four Arms, are you or are you not a spy for Hama?"

Geo could not read the expression that came over Snake's face. The boy shook his head not in denial but bewilderment. Suddenly he got up from the table, and ran from the room. Urson looked at the others. "Now don't tell me I hurt his feelings by asking."

"You didn't," said Geo, "but I may have. I keep on forgetting that he can read minds."

"What do you mean?" Urson asked.

"Just when you asked him that, a lot of things came together in my mind that would be pretty vicious for him if any of them were true."

"Huh?" asked Urson.

"I think I know what you mean," said Iimmi.

"I still—"

"It means that he is a spy," exclaimed Geo, "and among other things, he was probably lying about the radio back at the city. And that cost me my arm."

"Why, the . . ." began Urson, and then looked down the hall where Snake had disappeared.

They didn't eat much more. When they got up, Urson felt sleepy and was shown back to his room.

"May I show my friend what you showed me?" Iimmi asked the Priestess when she returned. "He is also a student of rituals."

"Of course you may," smiled the Priestess. "However, as students of the rituals of Argo you show surprising ignorances."

"As I tried to explain," said Iimmi, "we come from a land where the rituals have changed a great deal with time."

"Surely not that much," said the Priestess, smiling. "But you make such a fuss. These are only our commonest prayers. They do not even touch the subjects of magic." She led them down the hall. "And your amazement quite amazes me. Yours must be a young and enthusiastic people."

A door opened and they entered another room similar to the one in which Geo had awakened. As she was about to leave, Iimmi said, "Wait. Can you tell us how to leave the room ourselves?"

"Why would you want to leave?" she asked.

"For exercise," offered Geo, "and to observe the working of the convent. Believe us; we are true students of Argo's religion."

"Simply press the wall with your hand, level at your waist, and the door will open. But you must not wander about the convent. Rites which are not for your eyes are being carried out. . . . Not for your eyes," she repeated. "Strange, this phrase has never left our language. Suddenly, confronted by people who can see, it makes me feel somehow . . ." She paused. "Well, that is how to leave the room."

She stepped out. The door closed.

"Here," said Iimmi, "this is what I wanted to show you." On his bed was a pile of books, old, but legible. Geo flipped through a few pages. Suddenly he looked up at Iimmi.

"Hey, what are they doing with *printed* books?"

"Question number one," said Iimmi. "Now, for question number two. Look here." He reached over Geo's shoulder and hastened him to one page.

"Why it's the . . ." began Geo.

"You're damn right it is," said Iimmi.

"*Hymn To The Goddess Argo,*" Geo read aloud. And then:

> "*Forked in the eye of the bright ash*
> *there the heart of Argo broke*
> *and the hand of the goddess would dash*
> *through the head of flame and smoke.*
>
> *Burn the grain speck in the hand*
> *and batter the stars with singing.*
> *Hail the height of a man,*
> *also the height of a woman.*
>
> *Take from the tip of the sea*
> *salt and sea-kelp and gold.*
> *Vision, a shaft through the brain,*
> *and the terror of time is old.*
>
> *Salt to scour the tongue,*
> *salt on the temple floor,*
> *sea-kelp to bind up my hair*
> *and set forth for gold once more.*
>
> *The eyes have imprisoned a vision,*
> *the ash-tree dribbles with blood.*
> *Thrust from the gates of the prison,*
> *smear the yew-tree with mud.*

"That must be the full version of the poem I found the missing stanza to back in the library at Leptar."

"As I was saying," said Iimmi. "Question number two: what is the relation between the rituals of Hama and the old rituals of Argo? Apparently this particular branch of the religion of the Goddess underwent no purge."

"If the librarian at Olcse Ohwn could see these," breathed Geo, "he'd probably pick them up with long tongs, put his hand over his eyes, and carry them to the nearest fire."

Iimmi looked puzzled. "Why?"

"Don't you remember? These are forbidden. One of the reasons they were destroyed was because nobody was supposed to know about them."

"I wonder why?" Iimmi asked.

"That's question number three. How did you get hold of them?"

"Well," said Iimmi, "I sort of suspected they might be here. So I just asked for them."

"And I think I've got some answers to those questions."

"Fine. Go ahead."

"We'll start from three, go back to one, and then on to two. Nice and orderly. Why wasn't anybody supposed to know about the rituals? Simply because they *were* so similar to the rituals of Hama. You remember some of the others we found in the abandoned temple? If you don't, you can refresh your memory right here. The two sets of rituals run almost parallel, except for a name changed here, a color switched from black to white, a variation in the vegetative symbolism. I guess what happened was that when Hama's forces invaded Leptar five hundred years ago, it didn't take Leptar long to discover the similarity. From the looks of the City of New Hope, I think it's safe to assume that at one time or another, say five hundred years ago, Aptor's civilization was far highter than Leptar's, and probably wouldn't have had too hard a time beating her in an invasion. So when Leptar captured the first jewel, and somehow did manage to repel Aptor, the priests of Leptar assumed that the safest way to avoid infiltration by Hama and Aptor again would be to make the rituals of Argo as different as possible from the ones of their enemy, Hama. There may have been a small following of Hama in Leptar before the invasion, but all traces of it were destroyed with the rituals."

"Why do you say that?"

"Well, there's apparently a small peaceful following of Argo here in Aptor. There may have even been trade between the two, which is why the stories of Aptor survive among sailors. The ghouls, the flying things, they parallel the stories the sailors tell too closely to be accidents. How many men do you think have been shipwrecked on Aptor and gotten far enough into the place to see what we've seen, and then gotten off again to tell about it?''

"I can think of two," said Iimmi.

"Huh?"

"Snake and Jordde," answered Iimmi. "Remember that Argo said there had been spies from Aptor before. Jordde is definitely one, and I guess so is Snake."

"That fits with Rule Number One." He got up from the bed. "Come on. Let's take a walk. I want to see some sunlight." They went to the wall. Geo pressed it and the triangular panel slipped back.

When they had rounded four or five turns of hallway, Geo said, "I hope you can remember where we've been."

"I've got a more or less eidetic memory for directions," Iimmi said.

Suddenly the passage opened onto steps, and they were looking out upon a huge, white concourse. Down a set of thirty marble steps priestesses filed below, their heads fixed blindly forward. Each woman's hand rested on the shoulder of the one ahead of her. There were over a hundred, but the lines never collided. One row would merely pause for another to pass, and then begin to glide forward again. The silence and the whiteness were dreamlike.

At the far end was a raised dais with a mammoth statue of a kneeling woman, sculptured of the same effulgent, argic stone. "Where do these women come from?" whispered Iimmi. "And where do they keep the men?"

Geo shrugged.

A priestess came across the temple floor now, alone. She reached the bottom steps, and as she began to ascend, Geo recognized her as the one in charge. She climbed directly toward them, stopped in front of them and said, almost inaudibly, "Gentlemen, you are disturbing the hour of meditation. I asked you not to wander indiscriminately about the convent. Please return with me."

As she glided past, Geo and Iimmi frowned at one another. After they had rounded a few corners, Geo said, "Excuse me, ma'am, we didn't mean to be disrespectful, but we are used to natural day and night. We need fresh air, green things. This underground whiteness is oppressive and makes us restless. Could you show us a way into the open?''

"No," returned the blind Priestess quietly. "Besides, night is coming on and you are not creatures who relish darkness.''

"The night air and the quiet of evening are refreshing to us," countered Iimmi.

"What do you know of the night?" answered the Priestess with faint cynicism in her low voice. Now they reached the chapel where the friends had first met after their rescue.

"Perhaps," suggested Geo, "you could talk to us a while, then. There are many things we would like to know.''

` The Priestess turned, sighed softly, and said, "Very well. What would you like to talk about?''

"For instance," said Geo, "what can you tell us about the Dark God Hama?''

The blind Priestess shrugged, and sat on one of the benches. "There is little to say. Today he is a fiction; he does not exist. There is only Argo, the One White Goddess.''

"But we've heard—''

"You were at his abandoned temple," said the Priestess. "You saw yourselves. That is all that is left of Hama. Ghouls prey on the dust of his dead saints.''

Iimmi and Geo looked at each other again, puzzled. "Are you sure?'' Geo asked.

"Perhaps," mused the Priestess, "somewhere behind the burning mountain a few of his disciples are left. But Hama is dead in Aptor. You have seen the remains of his city, the City of New Hope. You have also been the first ones to enter it and return in nearly five hundred years.''

"Is that how long the city has been in ruin?'' asked Geo.

"It is.''

"What can you tell us about the city?''

The Priestess sighed again. "There was a time," she began, "generations ago, when Hama was a high god in Aptor. He had many temples, monasteries, and convents devoted to him. We had few. Except for these religious sanctuaries, the land was barbaric, wild, uninhabitable for the most part. There had once been cities in Aptor, but these had been destroyed even earlier by the Great Fire. All that we had was a fantastic record of an unbelievable time before the rain of flame, of tremendous power, vast science, and a towering, though degenerate, civilization. These records were extensive, and almost entirely housed within the monasteries. Outside, there was only chaos; half the children were born dead, and the other half deformed. Because of the monstrous races that sprang up over the island now as a reminder to us, we decided the magic contained in these chronicles was evil, and must never be released to the world again. But the priests of Hama, however, did not come to the same decision. They decided to use the information in these chronicles, spread it to the people; they were sure they would not commit the same mistakes that had brought the Great Fire. They opened the books, and a dream materialized from their pages, and that dream was the City of New Hope, which sits in ruin now on the far shore. They made giant machines that flew. They constructed immense boats which could sink·into the sea and emerge hundreds of miles away in another harbor in another land. They even harnessed for beneficial use the fire metal, uranium, which had brought such terror to the world before, and had brought down the flames.''

"But they made the same mistake as the people before the Great Fire made?" suggested Iimmi.

"Not exactly," said the Priestess. "That is, they were not so stupid as to misuse the fire metal which ravaged the world so harshly before. History is cyclic, not repetitive. A new power was discovered that dwarfed the significance of the fire metal. It could do all that the fire metal could do, and more efficiently: destroy cities, or warm chill huts in winter; but, it could also work on men's minds. They say, that before the Great Fire, men wandered the streets of the cities terrified that flames might descend on them any moment and destroy them. They panicked, brought flimsy, useless contraptions to guard themselves from the fire.

"Geo, Iimmi, have you any idea how terrifying it would be to know that while walking the streets, at any moment, your mind might be snatched from you, raped, violated, and left broken in your own skull? Only three of these instruments were constructed. But the moment their existence was made known by a few fantastic demonstrations, the City of New Hope began the swerve down the arc of self-destruction. It lasted for a year, and ended with the wreck you escaped from

last night. During that year invasions were launched on the
backward nations across the sea with whom, months before,
there had been friendly trade. Civil wars broke out and
internal struggles caused the invasions to fall back to the
homeland. The instruments were lost, but not before the bird
machines had even destroyed the City of New Hope itself.
The house of the fire metal was broken open to release its
death once more. For a hundred years after the end, say our
records, the city flamed with light from the destroyed power-
house. And mechanically, to this day, our instruments tell us,
the lights along its elevated highways flare at sunset, as if
dead hands were there to operate them. During the first
hundred years more and more of our number were born blind
because of the sinking fire in the city. At last we moved
underground, but it was too late." She rose from her seat.
"And so you see, Hama destroyed himself. Today, loyal to
Argo, are all the beasts of the air, of the land . . ."

"And of the waters," concluded Iimmi.

She smiled again. "Again, not exactly. We have had
some trouble with a certain race of aquatic creatures, as well
as the ignorant ghouls. Right after the Great Fire, evolution-
ary processes were tremendously turned awry, and we believe
this is how these creatures developed. For some reason we
cannot control them. Perhaps their intelligence is too elemen-
tal even to respond to pain. But all the rest are loyal," she
said. "All."

"What about the . . . the three instruments?" Geo asked.
"What happened to them?"

The blind Priestess turned to him. "Your guess," she
said, smiling, "is as good as mine." She turned and glided
from the room.

When she left, Geo said, "Something is fishy."

"But what is it?" asked Iimmi.

"For one thing," said Geo; "we know there is a Temple
of Hama. From the dream I would say that it's just about the
size and organization of this place."

"Just how big is this place anyway?"

"Want to do some more exploring?"

"Sure. Do you think she does know about Hama but was
just pretending?"

"Could be," said Geo. They started off down another corridor. "That bit about going into men's minds with the jewels . . ."

"It gives me the creeps."

"It's a creepy thing to watch," said Geo. "Argo used it on Snake the first time we saw her. It just turns you into an automaton."

"Then it really is our jewels she was talking about."

Stairs cut a white tunnel in the wall before them, and they mounted, coming finally to another corridor. For the first time they saw doors in the wall. "Hey," said Geo, "maybe one of these goes outside."

"Fine," said Iimmi. "This place is beginning to get me." He pushed open a door and stepped in. Except for the flowing white walls, it duplicated in miniature the basement of the New Edison building. Twin dynamos whirred and the walls were laced with pipes.

"Nothing in here," said Iimmi.

They tried a door across the hall. In this room sat a white porcelain table and floor-to-ceiling cases of glittering instruments. "I bet this is the room your arm came off in," Iimmi said.

"Probably."

The next room was different. The glow was dimmer, and there was dust on the walls. Geo ran his finger over it and looked at the gray crescent left on the bleached flesh. "This looks a little more homey."

"This is what you call homey?" Iimmi gestured toward the opposite wall. Two screens leaned from the face of a metal machine. A few dials and meters were set beneath each rounded-rectangle of opaque glass. In front was a stand which held something like a set of binoculars and what looked like a pair of earmuffs.

"I bet this place hasn't been used since before these girls went blind."

"It looks it," Iimmi said.

Geo stepped up to one of the screens, the one with the fewer dials on it, and turned a switch.

"What did you do that for?"

"Why not?" Suddenly a flickering of colored lights ran

over the screen, swellings of blue, green, scarlets. They blinked. "That's the first color I've seen since I've been here."

The colors grayed, dimmed, congealed into forms, and in a moment they were looking at a bare white room in which stood two barefoot young men. One was a dark Negro with pale hands. The other had an unruly shock of black hair and one arm.

"Hey!" Iimmi gestured: the figure on the screen gestured too. "That's us!" Geo walked forward and the corresponding figure advanced on the screen. He flicked a dial and the figures exploded into colors and then focused again into complete whiteness. "What's that?" asked Iimmi.

"We must be looking at a room with no people in it." Geo flicked the dial again. When the screen focused, they were looking at the dining room. Now a hundred or more women sat at the long tables, each bending and raising her blind face over bowls of red soup. In one corner, empty, was the table at which they had eaten. "I bet we could look into every room in the place." He switched the dial again. "Maybe we can find Urson and Snake." Two more rooms, then the great temple hall formed on the screen, empty save for the statue of Argo kneeling. As the next room passed, Geo called out, "Wait a minute!"

"What is it?"

In this room stood three of the blind women. On one wall was a smaller screen similar to the one in their own room. The women, of course, were oblivious to the picture, but the face on the screen had stopped Geo.

One of the women had on an earmuff apparatus and was talking into a small metal rod which she carried with her as she paced.

But the face! "Don't you recognize him?" demanded Geo.

"It's Jordde!" exclaimed Iimmi.

"They must have gotten in contact with our ship and are arranging to send us back."

"I wish I could hear what they're saying," said Iimmi.

Geo looked around and then picked up the metal earmuffs from the stand in front of the screen. "That's what she seems to be listening through," Geo said, referring to the Priestess in the picture. He fit them over his ears.

"Hear anything?" Iimmi asked.

Geo listened.

'. . . Yes, of course,' the Priestess was saying.

'She is set upon staying in the harbor for three more days, to wait out the week,' reported Jordde. 'I am sure she will not stay any longer. She is still bewildered by me, and the men have become uneasy and may well mutiny if she stays longer.'

'We will dispose of the prisoners this evening. There is no chance of their returning,' stated the Priestess.

'Detain them for three days, and I do not care what you do with them,' said Jordde. 'She does not have the jewels; she does not know my . . . our power; she will be sure to leave at the end of the week.'

'It's a pity we have no jewels for all our trouble,' said the Priestess. 'But at least all three are back in Aptor, and potentially within our grasp.'

Jordde laughed. 'And Hama never seems to be able to keep hold of them for more than ten minutes before they slip from him again.'

'Yours is not to judge either Hama or Argo,' stated the Priestess. 'You are kept on by us only to do your job. Do it, report, and do not trouble either us or yourself with opinions. They are not appreciated.'

'Yes, Mistress,' returned Jordde.

'Then, farewell until next report.' She flipped a switch and the picture on the little screen went gray.

Geo was turned from the big screen, now, and was just about to remove the hearing apparatus when he heard the Priestess say, 'Go; prepare the prisoners for the sacrifice of the rising moon. They have seen too much.' The woman left the room, Geo removed the phones, and Iimmi looked at him.

"What's the matter?"

Geo turned the switch that darkened the screen.

"When are they coming to get us?" Iimmi asked excitedly.

"Right now, probably," Geo said. Then, as best he could, he repeated the conversation he had overheard to Iimmi, whose expression grew more and more bewildered as Geo went on.

At the end the bewilderment suddenly flared into frayed indignation. "Why?" demanded Iimmi. "Why should we be sacrificed? What is it we've seen, what is it we know? This is the second time it's come close to getting me killed, and I wish to hell I knew what I was supposed to know?''

"We've got to find Urson and get out of here!"

"Hey, what's wrong?"

Indignation had turned into something else. Geo stood with his eyes shut tight and his face screwed up. Suddenly he relaxed. "I just thought out a message as loud as I could for Snake to get up here and to bring Urson if he's anywhere around.''

"But Snake's a spy for—"

"—for Hama," said Geo. "And you know something? I don't care." He closed his eyes again. After a few moments, he opened them. "Well, if he's coming, he's coming. Let's get going.''

"But why . . . ?" began Iimmi, following Geo out the door.

"Because I have a poet's feeling that some fancy mind reading may come in handy.''

They hurried down the hall, found the stairs, ducked down, and ran along the lower hall. Rounding a second corner, they emerged into the little chapel simultaneously with Urson and Snake.

"I guess I got through," said Geo. "Which way do we go?''

"Gentlemen, gentlemen," came a voice behind them.

Snake took off down one of the passages; they followed, Urson looking particularly bewildered.

The Priestess glided behind, calling softly, "Please, my friends, come back. Return with me.''

"Find out from her how the hell to get out of this place!" Geo bawled to Snake. The four armed boy darted up a sudden flight of stairs, turned, and ran up another. They came out in a hall, behind Snake.

The boy's four hands flew at the door handle, turning it carefully, this way, and back.

Two, three seconds.

Geo glanced back and saw the Priestess mount the head of the stairs and start toward them. Her white robes floated from her, brushing the walls.

The door came open, they broke through leaves, and

were momentarily in a huge field, surrounded by woods. The sky was pale with moonlight.

A hundred fifty yards across the field was a white statue of Argo. As they ran through the silver grass, doors opened in the base and a group of priestesses emerged and began to hurry toward them. Geo turned to look behind him. The blind Priestess had slowed, her face turned to the moon. Her hands went to her throat, she unclasped her robe, and the first layer fell behind her. As she came on, the second layer began to unfold, wet, leprously white, spreading from her arms, articulating along the white spines; then, with a horribly familiar shriek, she leaped from the ground and soared upward, white wings hammering the air.

They fled.

Dark forms shadowed the moon. The priestesses across the field joined her aloft in the moon-bleached night. She overtook the running figures, turned above them, and swooped. The moon lanced white on bared teeth. The breeze touched pale furry breasts, filled the bellying wings. Only the tiny, darting, blind eyes were red, rubies in a whirl of white.

Snake changed direction and fled towards the trees.

With only one arm, Geo found himself off balance. He nearly fell twice before he crashed into the bushes where the winged things could not follow. Branches raked his face as he followed the sound the others made. Once he thought he had lost them, but a second later he bumped against Iimmi, who had stopped behind Snake and Urson. Above the trees was a sound like beaten cloth, diminishing, growing, but constant as once more they began to tread through the tangled darkness.

"Damn..." sighed Iimmi, after a minute of walking.

"It's beginning to make sense," Geo said, his hand on Iimmi's shoulder. "Remember that man-wolf we met, and that thing in the city? The only thing we've met on this place that hasn't changed shape is the ghouls. I think most creatures on this Island undergo some sort of metamorphosis."

"What about those first flying things we met?" whispered Urson. "They don't change into anything."

"We have probably just been guests of the female of the species," said Geo. "I think perhaps that was what Snake was warning us against when he took us to see them in the barracks. He was trying to tell us that we might meet them again."

"You mean those others could have changed into men, too, if they wanted?" Urson asked.

"If they wanted," answered Geo. "But it was probably more convenient to stay outside the convent. They only come together for mating, more than likely."

"Which just might be what this ceremony of the rising moon is about," Iimmi observed. "The ones flying against the moon were the other kind, the men. You know there are sections over in Leptar where the female worshipers of Argo completely avoid the male members."

"That's what I was thinking of," said Geo. "It first dawned on me when they wouldn't let us eat with the women."

In front of them now appeared shiftings of silver light. Five minutes later, they were crouching at the edge of the trees, looking down over the rocks at the shimmering river.

"Into the water?" Geo asked.

Snake shook his head. *wait . . . inside their heads.*

A hand raised from the water. Wet and green, a foot or so from the shore, it turned, the chain and the leather thong dangling down the wrist: swinging there were two bright beads.

Iimmi and Geo froze. Urson said: "The jewels . . ."

Suddenly the big sailor sprang onto the rocks and ran toward the river's edge.

Three shadows, one white, two dark, converged above him, cutting the moonlight away. If Urson saw them, he did not stop.

Iimmi and Geo stood up.

Urson reached the shore, threw himself along the rock, swiped at the hand, and was covered by flailing wings. The membranous sails splashed in the water, there were shrieks, and one white wing arced high, then flapped down again. Two seconds later, Urson rolled from beneath the creatures still struggling half on land and half in the water. He staggered to his feet and started up the rocks again. He slipped, regained his footing, and came on, to fall into Geo's and Iimmi's arms.

"The jewels . . ." Urson breathed.

The struggle continued on the water. Something held them down, twisted at them. Suddenly, the creatures stilled. Like great leaves, the three forms drifted apart, caught in the current, and floated away from the rocks.

Then two more forms bobbed to the surface, faces down, rocking gently, backs slicked wet and green.

"But those were the ones who..." Geo began. "Are they dead?" His face suddenly hurt a little, with something like the pain of verging tears.

Snake nodded.

"Are you sure?" asked Iimmi. His voice was slow.

their ... thoughts ... have ... stopped ... Snake said.

Crouching in front of them, Urson opened his scarred hands. The globes blazed through the leaves. The chain and the wet thong hung from his palm to the ground. "I have them..." he whispered. "...The jewels!"

CHAPTER NINE

Snake picked up the beads from the calloused palm, placed one around Geo's neck, one around Iimmi's. Urson watched the jewels rise.

Then they turned into the forest; the sound of wings had stopped.

"Where do we go now?" Urson asked.

"We follow Rule Number One," said Geo. "Since we know Hama does have a temple somewhere, we try to find it, get the third jewel, and rescue Argo Incarnate. Then we get back to the ship."

"In three days?" asked Urson. "Where do we start looking?"

"The Priestess said something about a band of Hama's disciples behind the fire mountain. That must mean the volcano we saw from the steps in the City of New Hope." Geo turned to Snake. "Did you read her mind enough to know if she was telling the truth?"

Snake nodded.

Iimmi thought a moment. "Since the river is that way . . . we should head"—he turned and pointed—"in that direction."

They fixed their stride now and started through the pearly leaves.

"I still don't understand what was going on back at the convent," Iimmi said. "Were they really priestesses of Argo? And what was Jordde doing?"

"I'd say yes on the first question, and guess that Jordde was a spy for them for an answer to the second."

"But what about Argo . . . I mean Argo on the ship?" asked Iimmi. "And what about Snake here?"

"Argo on the ship apparently doesn't know about Argo on Aptor," said Geo. "That's what Jordde meant when he reported to the priestesses that she was bewildered. She probably thinks just like we did, that he's Hama's spy. And this one here . . ." He gestured at Snake. "I don't know. I just don't know."

When the light failed, they lay together and tried to sleep. But minutes after they had settled, and the white disk dropped from the horizon, Geo suddenly called them up again. In the distant red glow they could make out the volcano's cone.

Snake made lights with the jewels, and they began to pick their way over the land, now barer and barer of vegetation. Broken trees leaned against broken boulders. The earth grew cindery. The air bore old and acrid ash.

Soon the red rim of the crater hung close above them.

"How near are we?" Urson asked.

"I think we've already started the slope," Geo said.

"Maybe we ought to stop before we go any further and wait till morning."

"We can't sleep here," mumbled Urson, pushing cinders with his foot. He stretched. "Besides, we don't have time to sleep."

Geo gazed up at the red haze. "I wonder what it's like to look into that thing in the middle of the night?" He began again and they followed. Twenty feet later Snake's light struck a lavid cliff that sheered up into the darkness. Going on beside it, they found a ledge that made an eighteen-inch footpath diagonally up the face.

"We're not going to climb that in the dark, are we?" asked Iimmi.

"Better than in the light," said Urson. "This way you can't see how far you have to fall."

Iimmi started up the lip of rock. Thirty feet on, instead of petering out and forcing them to go back, it broadened into level ground, and again they could go straight forward toward the red light above them.

"This is changeable country," Urson muttered.

"Men change into animals," said Iimmi; "jungles turn to mountains."

Geo reached up and felt the stub of his arm in the dark. "I've changed too, I guess.

"Change is neither merciful nor just," he recited:
"They say Leonard of Vinci put his trust
  in faulty paints: Christ's Supper turned to dust."

"What's that from?" Iimmi asked.

"Another one of my bits of original research," Geo explained. "It comes from a poem dating back before the Great Fire. I found it when I was doing research in the tombs."

"Who was Leonard of Vinci?" Iimmi asked.

"An artist, perhaps another poet or painter," said Geo. "I'm not really sure."

"Who's Christ?" Urson asked.

"Another god."

There were more rocks now, and Geo had to brace his stub against the wall fissure and hoist himself up with his good hand. The igneous points were sharp on his palm. The lights wavered from time to time as Snake transferred them from this hand to that, as he climbed at the lead. The boy rounded another jutting and the crags sent double shadows slipping down.

Reaching a fairly level spot, they turned to look behind them. They were standing on the brim of a bowl of blackness. The sky was starry, and lighter than the plate of velvet vegetation circling before them. They turned again and continued.

Through the night the glowing rim dropped. With it came a breeze that pushed sulfur powder through their hair and made their nostrils sting.

"Maybe we should go around and approach it from the other side," Urson suggested. "That way the wind won't be so bad."

They set their climb at an angle, now; soon the wind fell, and they could head straight up again.

The earth became scaly and rotten under their feet. Fatigue tied knots high in their guts so that what was in their stomachs hung like stone.

"I didn't realize how big the crater was," Iimmi said.

So much nearer the red glow, cut off at the bottom by the curve of the edge, took up a quarter of the sky.

"Maybe it'll erupt on us," Urson muttered. He added, "I'm thirsty. If Hama is supposed to be behind the volcano, couldn't we have gone around instead of over it?"

"We're this far," said Iimmi. "Why turn back now?" A scab of shale skittered from under his foot. The wind shifted again and they were forced to skirt further around the crater.

"I hope you're keeping track how far off course we've gotten," Urson said.

"Don't worry," said Iimmi.

The glow from the jewels in Snake's hands showed pale yellow growths about them on the slope like miniature bulbous cactuses. Some of them whistled. "What are they?" Urson asked.

"Sulfur cones," said Iimmi. "Deposits of sulfur get caught under the surface, are heated, and make little volcanoes all by themselves."

After another comparatively level stretch, they began the final ascent over veins of rock and twisting trails that took them up the last hundred feet.

Once Urson looked back and saw Geo had stopped some twenty feet behind them at a niche in the ledge. Urson turned around and scrambled back. There was sweat on the boy's upturned face as the big sailor came toward him, gleaming in the red flicker.

"Here," Urson said. "Give me a hand."

"I can't," Geo whispered. "I'll fall."

Urson reached down, caught the boy around the chest, and hoisted him over the rock. "Take it easy. You don't have to race with anybody." Together they made their way after the others.

Iimmi and Snake cleared the crater rim first; Urson and Geo joined them on the pitted ledge. Together they looked into the volcano as red and yellow light splashed their chests and faces.

Gold dribbled the internal slope. Tongues of red rock lapped the sides, and the swirling basin belched brown blobs of smoke which rose up the far rocks to spill the brim a radian away.

White explosions in the white rock roared below them.

Pylons of blue flame leaped, then sank back. Trails of light webbed the crater's walls. At places ebon cavities jeweled the rock.

Wind fingered the watchers' hair.

Geo saw her first, two hundred feet along the rim. Her veils, bloodied by the flame, blew about her as she approached. Geo pointed to her. The others looked up.

She stood very straight. White hair snapped at the side of her head in the warm wind. Firelight and shadow fell deeply in the wrinkles of her face. As she neared them, light ran like liquid down the side of her winded robe. She smiled and held out her hand.

"Who are you?" Geo suddenly asked.

"Shadows melt in light of sacred laughter,"

recited the woman in a sure, low voice.

"Hands and houses shall be one hereafter."

She paused. "I am Argo Incarnate."

"But I thought . . ." Iimmi started.

"What did you think?" inquired the elderly woman, gently.

"Nothing," said Iimmi.

"He thought you were a lot younger," Urson said. "We're supposed to take you home." Suddenly he pointed into the volcano. "Say, this isn't any of that funny light like back in the city that burned our hands, only this time it made you old?"

She glanced down the crater wall. "This is natural fire," she assured them, "a severed artery of the earth's burning blood. But wounds are natural enough."

Geo shifted his feet and rubbed his stump. "We were supposed to take the daughter of the present Argo Incarnate and return with her to Leptar," he explained.

"There are many Argos," smiled the woman. "The Goddess has many faces. You have seen quite a few since you arrived in this land."

"I guess we have," Urson said.

"Are you a prisoner of Hama?" asked Iimmi.

"I am with Hama."

"We are supposed to secure the third jewel and bring it back to the ship. We don't have much time. . . ."

"Yes," said Argo.

"Hey, what about that nest of vampires down there?" Urson said, thumbing viciously toward the black behind them. "They said they worshiped Argo. What have you got to do with them? I don't trust anything on this place very much."

"The nature of the Goddess is change." She looked sadly down the slope. "From birth, through life, to death"— she looked back up at them—"to birth again. As I said, Argo has many faces. You must be very tired."

"Yes," said Geo.

"Then come with me. Please." She turned, and began to walk back along the rim. Snake and Iimmi started after her, then came Geo and Urson.

"I don't like any of this," the big sailor whispered to Geo as they followed. "Argo doesn't mean the same thing in this land as she does in Leptar. There's nothing but more trouble to come out of this. She's leading us into a trap, I tell you. I say the best thing to do is take the jewels we have, turn around, and get the hell out of here. I tell you, Geo—"

"Urson."

"Huh?"

"Urson, I'm very tired."

They walked silently for a few steps more. Then Urson heaved up a disgusted breath, and put his arm around Geo's shoulder. "Come on," he grunted, supporting Geo against his side as they progressed along the rocky ledge, following Argo.

She turned down a trail that dropped into the crater. "Walk carefully here," she said as they turned into the huge pit.

"Something's not right," Urson said softly. "It's a trap, I tell you. How does that thing go? I could use it now: *Calmly, brother bear . . .*"

>   *"Calm the winter sleep,"*

continued Geo:

>   *"Fire shall not harm . . ."*

"Says who," mumbled Urson, glancing into the bowl of flame.

Geo went on:

>   *"Water not alàrm.*
>   *While the current grows,*
>   *amber honey flows,*
>   *golden salmon leap."*

"Like I once said before," muttered Urson: "In a—"

"In here," announced Argo. They turned into one of the caves that pocked the inner wall. "No," she said to Snake, who was about to use the jewels for illumination. "They have been used too much already."

With a small stick from a pocket in her robe, she struck a flame against the rock, then raised it to an ornate, branching petrolabra that hung from the stone ceiling by brass chains. Flame leaped from oil cup to oil cup, from the hand of a demon to a monkey's mouth, from a nymph's belly to a satyr's head. Chemicals in the cups caused each flame to burn a different color: green, red, blue, and orange light filled the small chapel and played on the polished benches. On the altar were two statues of equal height: a man sitting, and a woman kneeling. Geo and Urson stared at the petrolabra.

"What is it?" Iimmi asked when he saw where their eyes were fixed.

"There's one of those things in Argo's cabin on board the ship," Geo said. "And look over there. Where did we see one of those before?" The opaque glass screen was identical to the one in the convent.

"Sit down," Argo said. "Please sit down."

They sank to the benches. The climb, once halted, knotted their calves and the low muscles on their backs.

"Hama has allowed you the privilege of a chapel even in captivity," commented Geo; "but I see you have to share your altar with him."

"But I am Hama's mother," smiled Argo.

Geo and Urson frowned.

"You yourselves know that Argo is the mother of all things, the begetter and bearer of all life. I am the mother of all gods as well."

"Those blind women," said Urson. "They aren't really your priestesses, are they? They wanted to kill us. I bet they were really dupes of Hama. . . ."

"It isn't so simple," replied Argo. "They are really worshipers of Argo, but as I said, I have many faces. Death as well as life is my province. The dwellers in that convent from which you escaped are a . . . how shall I say . . . a degenerate branch of the religion. They were truly blinded by the fall of the City of New Hope. To them, Argo is only death, the dominator of men. Not only is Argo the mother of Hama, she is his wife and daughter."

"Then it's like we figured," said Geo. "Jordde isn't a spy for Hama. He's working for the renegade priestesses of Argo."

"Yes," returned Argo, "except that 'renegade' is perhaps the wrong word. They believe that their way is correct."

"Then they must be responsible for all that was going on in Leptar, only somehow blaming it on Hama," said Geo. "They were probably just after the jewels, too. You don't look like a prisoner. You're here in league with Hama to prevent the priestesses of Argo from taking over Leptar."

"Nothing could be simpler," said the Goddess. "Unfortunately, you are wrong in nearly every other point."

"But then why did Jordde throw the jewel after us when he tore it from Argo's . . . I mean the other Argo's throat?"

"When he snatched the jewel from around my daughter's neck," explained Argo, "he threw it to the creatures of the sea because he knew they would take it back to Aptor. With it once again on the Island, the priestesses would have a better chance of getting it; my daughter, acting Argo Incarnate in the absence of her own daughter, does not know that what she is fighting is another face of Argo. As far as she is concerned, all her efforts are against the mischief Hama has caused, and truly caused in Leptar. But beyond these blind creatures is a greater enemy that she must vanquish."

"Hama . . . ?" began Iimmi.

"Greater than Hama," said old Argo. "It is herself. It is

hard for me to watch her and not occasionally call a word of
guidance. With the science here in Aptor it would not be
difficult. But I must refrain. Actually she has done well.
But there is much more to do. She has directed you well,
and assigned your tasks properly. And until now you have
carried them out well."

"She said we were to steal the final jewel from Hama
and return with you to the ship," said Geo. "Can you help us
with either of these things?"

"The moment I compliment you," laughed Argo, "you
completely confuse your mission. Once the jewel is stolen,
whom are you supposed to take back to Leptar?"

"Argo Incarnate," Urson said.

"You said that Argo back in the ship was your daughter," said Geo, "but she said you were *her* daughter. . . ."

Argo laughed. "When my granddaughter was . . . kidnapped
here to Aptor, I was already waiting for her. Look."

She turned a dial beneath the screen and lights flickered
over the glass: the sleeping girl had short red hair, a splash of
freckles over a blunt nose. Her hand curled in a loose fist near
her mouth. A white sheet covered the gentle push of adoles-
cent breasts. On the table beside her bed was a contraption
made of a U-shaped piece of metal mounted on a board, an
incomplete coil of wire, and a few more bits of metal, sitting
near a crumpled paper bag.

"That is my granddaughter," Argo said, switching off
the picture. "She is the one you must take back to the ship."

"How shall we steal the jewel?" asked Geo.

Argo turned to Snake. "I believe that was your task."
Then she looked around at the other three. "You will need
rest. After that you can see about the jewel and my granddaughter. Come with me, now. Pallets have been set up for
you in the far room, where you may sleep." She rose and led
them to a further chamber. The blankets lay over soft boughs.
Argo pointed to a trickle of water than ran from a basin carved
in the rock wall. "This stream is pure. You may drink from
it." She pointed to a burlap sack in the corner. "There is fruit
in there if you become hungry."

"Sleep!" Urson jammed his fists into the air, yawned.

As they settled, Argo said, "Poet?"

"Yes?" answered Geo.

"I know you are the most tired, but I must talk to you alone for a moment or two."

As Geo raised himself, Urson stood up, too. "Look," he said to Argo, "he needs the rest more than any of us. If you want to question him about rituals and spells, take Iimmi. He knows just as much as Geo."

"I need a poet," smiled Argo, "not a student. I need one who has suffered as he has. Come."

"Wait," Urson said. He picked the jewel from Geo's chest where Snake had returned it when they entered the chapel. "You better leave this with me."

Geo frowned.

"It may still be a trap," said Urson.

"Leave it with him," suggested Argo, "if it eases him."

Geo let the big hands lift the thong from his neck.

"Now come with me," said Argo.

They left the room and walked back through the chapel to the door. Argo walked to the entrance and looked down at the molten rock. Light sifted through her robe, leaving the darker outline of her body. Without turning, she spoke: "The fire is a splendid symbol for life, don't you think?"

"And for death. One of Aptor's fires burned my arm away."

She turned to him. "You and Snake have had the hardest time. Both of you have left flesh to rot in Aptor. I guess that involves you in this land. . . ." She paused. "You know, he had a great deal more pain than you. Do you know how he lost his tongue? I watched it all from this same screen inside the chapel, and could not help. Jordde jammed his knuckles into his jaws and, when the mouth came open, caught the red flesh with pincers that closed all the way through, and stretched it as far as it would go. Then he looped the tongue with a thin wire, and threw a switch. You don't know what electricity is, do you?"

"I have heard the word."

"When a great deal of it is passed through a thin wire, the wire becomes hot, white hot. And the white hot loop was tightened until the rope of muscle seared from the roasted stump. But the child had fainted already. I wonder if the young can really bear more pain."

"Jordde and the blind priestesses did this to him?"

"Jordde and some men on the boat that picked up the two of them from the raft on which they had left Aptor."

"Who is Jordde?" Geo asked. "Urson knew him before this as a First Mate. But Urson's story tells me nothing."

"I know the story," Argo said. "It tells you something, but something you would perhaps rather not hear." She sighed. "Poet, how well do you know yourself?"

"What do you mean?" Geo asked.

"How well do you know the machinery of a man, how he manages to function? That is what you will sing of if your songs are to become great."

"I still don't—"

"I have a question for you, a poetic riddle. Will you try to answer it?"

"If you will answer a question for me."

"Will you do your best to answer mine?" Argo asked.

"Yes."

"Then I will do my best to answer yours. What is your question?"

"Who is Jordde and why is he doing what he's doing?"

"He was at one time," Argo explained, "a very promising novice for the priesthood of Argo in Leptar, a scholar of myths and rituals like Iimmi and yourself. He also took to the sea to learn of the world. But his boat was wrecked; he and a few others were cast on Aptor's shore. They strove with Aptor's terrors as you did, and many fell. Two, however, a four armed cabin boy, whom you call Snake, and Jordde, were each exposed to the forces of Argo and Hama as you have been. One, in his strangeness, could see into men's minds. The other could not. Silently, one swore allegiance to one force, while one swore allegiance to the other. The second part of your question was *why*. Perhaps if you can answer my riddle, you can answer that part yourself. I do know that they were the only two who escaped. I do know that Snake would not tell Jordde his choice, and that Jordde tried to convince the child to follow him. When they were rescued, I know that the argument continued, and that Snake held back with childish tenacity both his decision and his ability to read minds, even under the hot wire and the pincers. The hot wire, incidentally, was something Jordde took back with him from the blind Priestess, according to him, to help the people of Leptar. It could have been a great use. But recently all he has done with the electricity is construct a larger weapon with it. Jordde became a staunch First Mate in a year's time. Snake became a waterfront thief. Both waited. Then, when the opportunity arose, both acted. Why? Perhaps you can tell me, Poet.''

"Thank you for telling me that much," Geo said. "What is your question?"

She glanced down at the flame once more and recited:

> *"By the dark chamber sits its twin,*
> *where the body's floods begin;*
> *and the two are twinned again,*
> *turning out and turning in.*
>
> *In the bright chamber runs the line*
> *of the division, silver, fine,*
> *diminishing along the lanes*
> *of memory to an inward sign.*
>
> *Fear floods in the turning room;*
> *Love breaks in the burning dome."*

"It is not one that I have heard before," Geo said. "I'm not even sure I know what the question is. I'm familiar with neither its diction nor style."

"I doubted very much you would recognize it," smiled Argo.

"Is it part of the pre-purge rituals of Argo?"

"It was written by my granddaughter," Argo said. "The question is: could you explain it to me?"

"Oh," said Geo. "I didn't realize . . ." He paused. "By the dark chamber sits its twin, moving in and out; and that's where the floods of the body begin. And they are twinned again. The heart?" he suggested. "The four chambered human heart? That's where the body's flood begins."

"I think that will do for part of the answer."

"The bright chamber," mused Geo. "The burning dome. The human mind, I guess. The line of division, running down the lane of memory . . . I'm not sure."

"You seem to be doing fairly well."

"Could it refer to something like 'the two sides of every question'?" Geo asked. "Or something similar?"

"It could," Argo said. "Though I must confess I hadn't thought of it in that way. But it is the last two lines that puzzle me."

"Fear floods in the turning room," repeated Geo. "Love breaks in the burning dome. I guess that's the mind and the heart again. You usually think of love with the heart, and fear with the mind. Maybe she meant that they both, the heart and the mind, have control over both love and fear."

"Perhaps she did." Argo smiled. "You must ask her . . . when you rescue her from the clutches of Hama."

"Does your granddaughter want to be a poet?" Geo asked.

"I'm not sure what she wants to be," Argo said. "It can be very trying. But you must go to sleep now. Tomorrow you will have to complete your mission."

"Thank you," Geo said, grateful for his dismissal. "I am . . . am very sleepy."

Before going back to the room to his companions, he looked once more into the volcano. Tongues of light licked the black rock. He turned away now and walked back into the darkness.

CHAPTER TEN

Dawn lay a-slant the crater's ridge. Argo pointed down the opposite slope. A black temple at the bottom of the slope sat among trees and lawns. "Hama's Temple," Argo said. "You have your task. Good luck."

They started down the cinder slope. It took them about thirty minutes to reach the first trees that surrounded the dark buildings and the vast gardens. As they crossed the first lip of grass, a sudden cluster of notes spilled from a tree.

"A bird," Iimmi said. "I haven't heard one since I left Leptar."

Bright blue and the length of a man's forefinger, a lizard ran halfway down the trunk of the tree. Its sapphire belly heaved in the early light; it opened its red mouth, its throat fluttered, and there was another burst of music.

"Oh well," said Iimmi. "I was close."

They walked further, until Geo mused: "I wonder why you always think things are going to turn out like you expect."

"Because when something sounds like that," declared Urson, "it's supposed to be a bird!" He shuddered. "Lizards!"

"It was a pretty lizard," said Geo.

"Echhh!" said Urson.

"Going around expecting things to be what they seem can get you in trouble . . . on this Island."

There was another sound from the grove beside them. They looked up. The man standing in the center raised his hand and said briskly, "Stop!"

They stopped.

123

He wore dark robes, and his white hair made a close helmet above his brown face.

Urson's hand was on his sword. Snake's hands were out from his sides.

"Who are you?" the man declared.

"Who are you?" Urson parried.

"I am Hama Incarnate."

They were silent. Finally Geo said: "We are travelers in Aptor. We don't mean any harm."

As the man moved forward, splotches of light from the trees slipped across his robe. "Come with me," Hama said. He turned and proceeded among the trees. They followed.

They entered the Temple garden. It was early enough in the morning so that the sunlight lapped pink tongues over the giant urns along the edges of the path. They reached the Temple.

The mirrors on the sides of the vestibule tossed images back and forth as they passed between. Beyond pillars of onyx spread the shiny floor of the Temple. On the huge altar sat an immense statue of a cross-legged man. In one monstrous black hand was a scythe. In the other, shafts of grain spired four stories toward the ceiling. Of the three eyes in the head, only the middle one was open.

As they passed, Hama looked at the jewels on Iimmi's and Geo's necks, and then up at the gazing eye. "The morning rites have not yet started," he said. "They will begin in a half hour. By then I hope to have divined your purpose in coming here."

At the other side of the hall they mounted a stairway. Above the door was a black circle dotted with three eyes. Just as they were about to go in, Geo looked around, frowned, and caught Iimmi's eye. "Snake?" he mouthed.

Iimmi looked around and shrugged. The boy was not with them.

The room contained screens like the ones in the volcanic chapel and at the convent of the blind priestesses. Other equipment also: a large worktable, and on one wall, a window through which they could see the Temple garden.

Hama faced them, apparently unaware of Snake's disappearance. As he closed the door now, he said: "You have come to oppose the forces of Aptor, am I right? You come to steal the jewel of Hama. You have come to kidnap Incarnate

Argo. Will you deny that is your purpose? Keep your hand off your sword, Urson! . . . I can kill you in a moment.''

She pushed her fist from under the sheet, squinched her eyes as tight as she could, and said, "Yahhhhhwashangnnn, damn!" Then again, "Damn! I'm sleepy." She rolled over and cuddled the pillow. Then she opened her eyes, one at a time, and lay watching the near-complete motor sitting on the table beside her bed. Her eyes closed.

And opened again. "I cannot afford to go back to sleep this morning," she said softly. "One, two, three!" then threw the covers off, sat up, flung her feet onto the stone floor, and jumped erect, blinking hard from the shock of flesh and cold rock. She put her teeth together and said loudly, "Gnnnnnnnnnnn," and stretched to tiptoe.

Then she collapsed on the bed and jammed her feet under the covers again. With thirty feet of one-and-a-half-inch brass pipe, she mused sleepily, I could carry heat from the main hot water line under the floor, which I would estimate to be about the proper surface area to keep these stones warm. Let me see; thirty feet of one-and-a-half-inch pipe has a surface area of 22/7 times 3/2 times 30 which is 990 divided by 7 which is . . . Then she caught herself. Damn, thinking about this to avoid thinking about getting up. She opened her eyes once more, put feet on the stone, and held them there while she scratched vigorously at her hair.

Then she went to the closet.

She pulled down a white tunic, wriggled into it, and tied the leather strap around her waist. Then she looked at the clock. "Yikes!" she said quietly, ran out the door, almost slammed it to behind her. But she whirled, caught it on her palms before it banged, then with ginger care closed it the final centimeter. Are you trying to get caught? she asked herself as she tiptoed to the next door.

She opened it and looked in. Dunderhead looks cute when he's asleep, she thought. The cord on the floor ran from under the table by the Priest's bed, over the stones, carefully following the zigzag crevices. The end lay in the corner of the door sill. You really couldn't see it if you weren't looking for it, which had more or less been the idea when she put it there last night before the priests returned from vespers. The far end was tied in a knot of her own invention to the electric plug of his alarm clock. Dunderhead had an annoying habit of resetting his clock every evening (in her plans for this morning she had catalogued all his habitual actions, this one observed three nights running, as she hung upside-down from the bulky stone portcullis outside his window) to make sure the red second hand still swept away the minutes.

She tugged on the string and saw it leap from the crevices to a straight line. It lifted from the floor as she drew tighter. The plug blipped quietly onto the floor, and the string went slack.

She pulled the string again until the slack left, and raised the end a few inches from the floor. With her free hand she plucked the cord and watched the vibration run up and down. The knot's invention was ingenious. At the vibration, two opposed loops shook away from a third, and a four millimeter length of rubber band that had been sewn in tightened and released a fourth loop from a small length of number four gauge wire with a holding tonsure of three quarters of a gram, and the opposing vibration returning up the cord loosed a similar apparatus on the other side of the plug. The knot fell away, and she wound the string quickly around her hand. She stood up and closed the door. The oiled lock was perfectly silent. In fact the doorknob was still just the slightest bit greasy, she noted. Careless.

She went back to her room. Sunlight from the high window fell over the table. Glancing at her own clock, she saw it was still very early in the morning. She took the parts of the motor up. "I guess we try you out today? No?" She grinned. "Yes!" She put the parts in the paper bag, strode out of the room, and slammed the . . . whirled and caught it once more. "Gnnnnnnn," she said. "*Do* you want to get caught?" Now she frowned. "Yes. And remember that too. Or you'll never get through it."

As she walked down the hall, she heard through one of the windows the chirp of a blue lizard from the garden. "Just the sound I wanted to hear." Her smile came back. "Good sign."

Turning into the Temple, she started down the side aisle. The great black columns passed her. Suddenly she stopped.

Something had moved between the columns on the other side, swift as a bird's shadow. At least she thought it had. "Remember," she reminded herself, "you have guilt feelings about this whole thing, you want to get caught, and you could very easily be manufacturing delusions to scare yourself out of going through with it." She passed two more columns. And saw it again. "Or," she went on, "you could be purposefully ignoring the very obvious fact that there is somebody over there. So watch it."

Then she saw it again; somebody, with no clothes on (for all practical purposes) was sneaking between the pillars. And he had four arms. That made her start to think of something else, but the thought as it arrowed toward recognition, suddenly got deflected, turned completely about, and jammed into her brain: he was staring directly at her, and she was afraid.

If he starts walking toward me, she thought, I'm going to be scared out of my ears. So I better start walking toward him. Besides, I want to see what he looks like. She left the columns. Glancing quickly both ways, she saw that the Temple was deserted save for them.

He's a kid, she thought, three-quarters of the way across. My age, she added, and again a foreign thought tried to intrude itself on her but never made it: he was coming toward her, now. At last he stopped before her. His muscles lay like wire under his brown skin; black hair massed low on his forehead, and his eyes gleamed deep beneath the black shrub of brows.

She gulped. "What are you doing here? Do you know somebody could catch you in here and get mad as hell? If somebody comes along, they might even think you were trying to steal Hama's eye." I shouldn't have said that, because he moved funny. "You better get out of here because everybody will be up here in a half hour for morning services."

At that news, he suddenly darted past her, and sprinted toward the altar.

"Hey!" she called and ran after him.

Snake vaulted the brass altar rail.

"Wait a minute!" she called, catching up. "Wait, will you!"

Snake turned as she slung her leg across the brass bar. "Look; so I gave away my hand. But that was only guilt feelings. You gave yours away too, though."

Snake frowned, tilted his head, then grinned.

"We'll help each other, see. You want it too, don't you?" She pointed up to the head of the statue towering above them. "So let's cooperate. I'll take it for a little while. Then you can have it." He was listening, she saw; she guessed her strategy was working. "We'll help each other. Shake on it?" She stuck out her right hand.

All four hands reached forward.

Whoops, she thought, I hope he's not offended. . . .

But the four hands grasped hers, and she added her left to the juncture. "All right. Come on. Now, I had all this figured out last night. We don't have much time. Let's go around . . ." But he reached out and took the coil of string from where she had stuck it in her belt. He walked to where the stalks of wheat spired from the altar base up through Hama's fist. With the twine in one hand, he grabbed a stalk with the other three and, hand over hand over hand, hoisted himself up to where the first broad metal leaves branched from the stalk. His dirty feet swung out frogwise; then he caught the stem with his toes and at last hoisted himself to the frond. He looked down at her.

"I can't climb up there," she said. "I don't have your elevation power."

Snake shrugged.

"Oh damn," she said. "I'll do it my way." She ran across the altar to the great foot of the statue. Because he sat cross-legged, Hama's foot was on his side. Using toes for steps, she clammered to the dark bulge of the deity's divine bunion. She made her way across the ankle, up the shin, back down the black thigh, till she stood at the crevice where the leg and torso met.

Out beyond the great knee, Snake regarded her from his perch in the groin of the yellow leaf. They were at equal height.

"Yoo-hoo!" She waved. "Meet you at the clavicle." Then she stuck her tongue out. The stylized ripples in Hama's loincloth afforded her another ten feet. The bulge in the contrastingly realistic belly of the god made a treacherous ledge along which she inched until she arrived at the cavernous navel. Her hands left wet prints on the black stone.

Glancing out, she saw that Snake had gotten to the next cluster of leaves.

The god's belly-button, from this intimate distance, revealed itself as a circular door, about five feet in diameter. She dried her hands on her blouse, and crouched before the door and began to work the combination. She missed the first number twice, dried her hands off, and began again. According to the plans in the main safe of the Temple (on which she had first practiced combination breaking) there was a ladder behind this door which led up into the statue. She remembered it clearly; and saved her life by doing so.

Because when she reached the second number, reversed the dial and felt the telltale click at the third, she pulled on the handle—and was nearly pushed from the ledge as the door swung. She grabbed at a handle as the stone slipped from under her feet.

She was hanging five feet out in the air over the sacred groin fifty feet below.

The first thing she tried, after closing her eyes and mumbling a few laws of motion, was to swing the door to. When she swung out, however, the door swung closed; and when she swung in, the door swung open. After a while, she just hung. She gave small thanks that she had dried her hands. When her arms began to ache, she wished that she hadn't, because then it would be over by now. She went over what she knew about taking judo falls. After closing her eyes, she perfunctorily attempted to reconstruct what she could of an ancient poem, about a young lady who had ended in a similar position, with the refrain, "Curfew must not ring tonight. . . ."

Then the door swung closed, and someone grabbed her around the waist. She didn't open her eyes, but felt her body pressed against the tilting stone. Her arms dropped tingling to her sides. The ligaments flamed with pain. Then pain dulled to throbbing, and she opened her eyes. "How the hell did you get down here?" she asked Snake. Snake helped her stagger through the open door. She stopped to rub her arms. "How did he know about the ladder?"

They stood at the bottom of the shaft. The ladder beside them rose into the darkness.

He looked at her with a puzzled expression.

"What is it?" she asked. "Oh, I'll be able to climb up there, never you worry. Hey, can you speak?"

Snake shook his head.

"Oh," she said. Something started at the edge of her mind again, something unpleasant. Snake had started up the ladder, which he had come down so quickly a minute ago. She glanced out the door, saw that the Temple was empty, pulled the door to, and followed.

They ascended into darkness. Time somehow got lost, and she was not sure if she had been climbing for ten minutes, or two, or twenty. Once she reached for a rung and her hand fell on nothing. The shock in the rhythm started her heart beating. Her arms were beginning to ache again, just slightly. She reached up for the next rung, and found it in its proper place. Then the next. And then again the next.

She started counting steps again, and when seventy-four, seventy-five, and seventy-six dropped below her, there was another missing rung. She reached above it, but there was none. She ran her hand up the edge of the ladder and found that it suddenly curved, depressingly enough, into the wall.

"Hey, you!" she whispered in the darkness.

Something touched her waist. "Gnnnnnggggg," she said. "Don't *do* that." It touched her on the leg, took hold of her ankle, and pulled. "Watch out," she said.

It pulled again. She raised her foot, and it was tugged sideways a good half meter and set on solid flooring. Then a hand (her foot was not released) took her arm, and another held her waist, and tugged. She stiffened for one instant before she remembered the number of limbs her companion had. She stepped off the ladder, sideways into the dark, afraid to put her other foot down lest she go headlong into the seventy-five foot plus shaft.

Holding her arm now, he led her along the tunnel. We should be going through the shoulder, she figured, remembering the plan.

They reached a steep incline. Now, down the upper arm, she recalled. The slope, without visual orientation, made her a little dizzy. She put her hand out and ran her fingers along the wall. That helped some.

"I feel like Euridice," she said aloud.

you . . . funny . . . an echoing sounded in her skull.

"Hey," she said. "What was that?" But the voice was silent. The wall turned abruptly and the floor leveled out. They were in a section of the passage now that corresponded roughly to the statue's radial artery. At the wrist, there was a light. They mounted a stairway, came out a trapdoor, and found themselves high in the Temple. Below them the great hall spread, vast, deep, and empty. Beside them, the stems of the bronze wheat stalks rose up through the fist on which they were standing and spired another fifty feet before breaking into clusters of grain. Beyond the dark, gargantuan chest, in the statue's other hand, the giant scythe leaned into shadow.

"Look," she said. "You follow me now." She started back along the top of the forearm, and climbed over the rippling biceps. They reached the shoulder and crossed the hollow above the collarbone, until they stood just below the scooping shell of the ear.

"You still have the string?" she asked him.

Snake handed it to her.

"I guess my bag is heavy enough." She took the paper bag she had stuffed into her belt, tied one end of the string around the neck. Then, holding the other, she heaved the cord up and over the ear. She got the other end of the string, knotted it as high as she could reach, and gave it a tug.

"I hope this works," she said. "I had it all figured out yesterday. The tensile strength of this stuff is about two hundred and fifty pounds, which ought to do for you and me." She planted her foot on the swell of the neck tendon, and in seven leaps she made it to the lobe of the ear. She swung around using the frontal wing as a pivot. Crouching in the trumpet, she looked down at the Snake. "Come on," she said. "Hurry up."

Snake joined her a moment later.

The ear was hollow, too. It led back into a cylindrical chamber which went up through the head of the god. The architect who had designed the statue had conveniently left the god's lid flipped. They climbed the ladder at the side of the passage, and emerged amid the tangle of pipes representing hair. Where the forehead began to slope dangerously forward, they could see the foreshortened nose and the brow of the statue's middle eye above that. There wasn't much of anything after that for the next few hundred feet until the base of the altar. "Now you really can be some help," she told him. "Hold onto my wrist and let me down. Slowly now. I'll get the jewel."

They grabbed wrists, and Snake's other three hands, as well as the joints of his knees, locked around the base of five pipes that sprouted around them.

Slowly she slid forward, until her free hand slipped on the stone and she dropped the length of their two arms and swung just above the statue's nose. The eye opened in front of her. The lid arched above her, and the white of the eye either side of the ebony iris shone faintly in the half darkness. At this distance, all the features of the statue lost their recognizable human character, and she was staring into concaved darkness. At the center of the iris, in a small hollow, sitting on the top of a metal support, was the jewel.

She reached her free hand toward it as she swung.

Somewhere a gong sounded. Light flooded over her. Looking up, she saw white sockets of light shining down into her own eyes. Panicking, she almost released Snake's wrist. But a voice in her head (hers or someone else's, she couldn't tell) rang out:

hold . . . on . . . damn . . . it . . .

She grabbed the jewel. The metal shaft in which the jewel had sat was not steady, and tilted as her hand came away. The tilting must have set off some clockwork mechanism, because the great lid above was slowly lowering over the ivory and ebony eye. She swung again at the end of the rope of bone and flesh; half-blinded by the lights above her, she looked over her shoulder, down into the Temple. She heard singing, the beginning of a processional hymn.

The morning rites had started!

Light glinted on the stone limbs of the god. Figures poured into the Temple, miniature and far away. They must see her! But the hymns, sonorous and gigantic, rose like flood water, and she suddenly thought that if she fell, she would drown in the sound of it.

Snake was pulling her up. Stone against her arm, against her cheek. She clenched her other fist tightly at her side. Another hand came down to help. Then another. Then she was lying among the metal pipes, and he was prying her fingers from his wrist. He tugged her to her feet, and for a moment she looked out over the crowded hall.

Nervous energy contracted coldly along her body, and the sudden sight of the great drop filled her eyes and her head. She staggered. Snake caught her and at last helped her back to the ladder. "We've got it!" she said to him before they started down. She breathed deeply. Then she checked in her palm to see if it was still there. It was. Again she looked out over the people. Light on the upturned faces made them look like pearls on the dark floor. Exaltation suddenly burst in her shoulders, flooded her legs and arms, and for a moment washed the pain away. Snake, with one hand on her shoulder, was grinning. "We've got it!" she said again.

They went down the ladder inside the statue's skull. Snake preceded her out the ear. He reached around, caught the cord, and let himself down to the shoulder.

She hesitated, then put the jewel in her mouth, and followed him. Standing beside him once more, she removed it and rubbed her shoulders. "Boy, am I going to have some charley-horse by tomorrow," she said. "Do me a favor and untie my bag for me?"

Snake untied the parcel from the end of the cord, and together they climbed down the biceps and back over the forearm to the trapdoor in the wrist.

She glanced down at the worshipers. "I wonder which one is old Dunderhead?" But Snake was taking the jewel from her hand. She let him have it, and watched him raise it up above his head.

He raised the jewel and the pearls disappeared as heads bent all through the Temple.

"That's the ticket!" Argo grinned. "Come on." But Snake did not go into the tunnel. Instead he walked around the fist, took hold of one of the bronze wheat stems, and slid down through an opening between thumb and forefinger. "That way?" asked Argo. "Oh well, I guess so. You know I'm going to write an epic about this. In alliterative verse. You know what it is, alliterative verse . . . ?"

But Snake had already gone. She followed him, clutching the great stems with her knees. He was waiting for her at the leaves. Nestled there, they gazed once more at the fascinated congregation.

Again Snake held aloft the jewel, and again heads bowed. The hymn began to repeat itself, individual words lost in the sonority of the hall. The tones drew out, beat against themselves in echo, filled up their ears, made her wrists and the back of her neck chill. They started down the last of the stem, coming quickly. When they stood at last on the base, she put her hand on his shoulder and looked across the altar rail. The congregation pressed close, although she did not recognize an individual face. The mass of people stood there, enormous and familiar. As snake started forward, holding up the jewel, the people fell back. Snake climbed over the altar rail, then helped her over.

Her shoulders were beginning to hurt now, and the enormity of the theft ran chills up and down, up and down her back. The altar steps, as she put her foot down, were awfully cold.

They started forward again, and the last note of the hymn echoed to silence, filling the hall with the roaring hush of hundreds breathing.

Simultaneously, she and Snake got the urge to look back at the height of Hama behind them. All three eyes were shut firmly. A hundred dark robes rustled about them as they started forward again.

There was a spotlight on them, she realized. That was why the people, beyond the circular effulgence around them, seemed so dim. Blood pulsed at the bottom of her tongue. They walked forward, into shadowed faces, into parting cloaks and robes.

The last of the figures stepped aside from the Temple door, and she could see the sunlight out in the garden. They stood a moment. Snake held high the jewel. Then they burst from the door and over the bright steps.

The hymn began again behind them, as if their departure were a signal. Music poured after them. When they reached the bottom step, they whirled, like beasts, expecting the congregation to come welling darkly out after them.

There was only the music. It flowed into the light, washed around them, a transparent river, a sea.

"Freeze the drop in the hand,
and break the earth with singing.
Hail the height of a man,
also the height of a woman."

Over the music they heard a brittle chirping from the trees. Fixed with fear, they watched the Temple door. No one came out. Snake suddenly stood back and grinned.

She scratched her red hair, shifted her weight, and looked at Snake. "I guess they're not coming." She sounded almost disappointed. Then she giggled. "I guess we got it."

"Don't move," repeated Hama Incarnate.

"Now look . . ." began Urson.

"You are perfectly safe," the god continued, "unless you do anything foolish. You have shown great wisdom. Continue to show it. I have a lot to explain to you."

"Like what?" asked Geo.

"I'll start with the lizard." The god smiled.

"The what?" asked Iimmi.

"The singing lizards," said Hama. "You walked through a grove of trees just a few minutes ago. You had just been through the most frightening time in your lives. Suddenly you heard a singing in the trees. What was it?"

"I thought it was a bird," Iimmi said.

"But why a bird?" asked the god.

"Because that's what a bird sounds like," stated Urson impatiently. "Who needs an old lizard singing to them on a morning like this?"

"Your second point is much better than your first," said the god. "You do not need a lizard, but you did need a bird. A bird means spring, life, good luck, cheerfulness. You think of a bird singing and you think thoughts that men have been thinking for thousands upon thousands of years. Poets have written of it in every language, Catullus in Latin, Keats in English, Li Po in Chinese, Darnel 2X4 in New English. You expected a bird because after what you had been through, you needed to hear a bird. Lizards run from under wet rocks, scurry over gravestones. A lizard is not what you needed."

"So what do lizards have to do with why we're here'?" demanded Urson.

"Why are you here?" repeated the god, subtly changing Urson's question. "There are many reasons, I am sure. You tell me some of them."

"You have done wrongs to Argo . . . at least to Argo of Leptar," Geo explained. "We have come to undo them. You have kidnapped the young Argo, as well as her grandmother, apparently. We have come to take her back. You have misused the jewels. We have come to take the last one from you."

Hama smiled. "Only a poet could see the wisdom in such honesty. I thought I might have to wheedle to get that much out of you."

"It was pretty certain you knew that much already," Geo said.

"True." Then his tone changed. "Do you know how the jewels work?"

They shook their heads.

"They are basically very simple mechanical contrivances which are difficult in execution but simple in concept. I will explain. Human thoughts, it was discovered after the Great Fire during the first glorious years of the City of New Hope, did not produce waves similar to radio waves; but the electrical synapse pattern, it was found, could affect radio waves, in the same way a mine detector reacts to the existence of metal."

"Radio?" Geo said.

"That's right," Hama said. "Oh, I forgot. You don't know anything about that at all. I can't go through the whole thing now. Suffice it to say each of the jewels contains a carefully honed crystal which is constantly sending out beams that can detect these thought patterns. Also the crystal acts like both a magnifying glass and a mirror, and reflects and magnifies the energy from the brain into heat or light or any other kind of electromagnetic radiation—there I go again—so that you can send great bolts of heat with them, as you have seen done.

"But the actual workings of them are not important. And their ability to send heat out is only their secondary power. Their primary import is that they can be used to penetrate the mind. Now we come to the lizards."

"Wait a minute," Geo said. "Before we get to the lizards. Do you mean they go into minds like Snake does?"

The god went on. "Like Snake," he said. "But different. Snake was born with the ability to transmute the brain patterns of his thoughts to others; in that he has a power something like the jewels, but nowhere as strong. But with the jewels, you can jam a person's thoughts—"

"Just go into his mind and stop him from thinking?" asked Iimmi.

"No," said the god. "Conscious thought is too powerful. Otherwise, you would stop thinking every time Snake spoke to you. It works another way. How many reasons does a man have for any single action?"

They looked at him uncomprehendingly.

"Why, for example, does a man pull his hand from a fire?"

"Because it hurts," said Urson. "Why else?"

"Yes, why else?" asked Hama.

"I think I see what you mean," said Geo. "He also pulls it out because he knows that outside the fire his hand isn't going to hurt. Like the bird, I mean the lizard. One reason we reacted like we did was because it sounded like a bird. The other reason was because we wanted to hear a bird just then. The man pulls his hand out because the fire hurts, *and* because he wants it not to hurt.

"In other words," Geo summarized, "there are at least two reasons for everything."

"Exactly," explained Hama. "Notice that one of these reasons is unconscious. But with the jewel, you can jam the unconscious reason; so that if a man has his hand in a fire, you can jam his unconscious reason of wanting it to stop hurting. Completely bewildered, and in no less pain, he will stand there until his wrist is a smoking nub."

Geo reached over and felt his severed arm.

"Dictators during the entire history of this planet have used similar techniques. By not letting the people of their country know what conditions existed outside their boundaries, they could get the people to fight to stay in those conditions. It was the old adage: Convince a slave that he's free, and he will fight to maintain his slavery. Why does a poet sing? Because he likes music; and because silence frightens him. Why does a thief steal? To get the goods from his victim; also to prove that his victim cannot get him. . . ."

"That's how Argo got Snake back," Geo said to Urson. "I see now. He was just thinking of running away, and she jammed his desire not to get caught; so he had nothing to tell him in which direction to run. So he ran where she told him, straight back to her."

"That's right," Hama said. "But something else was learned when these jewels were invented. Or rather a lesson which history should have taught us thousands of years ago was finally driven home. No man can wield absolute power over other men and still retain his own mind. For no matter how good his intentions are when he takes up the power, his alternate reason is that freedom, the freedom of other people and ultimately his own, terrifies him. Only a man afraid of freedom would want this power, or could conceive of wielding it. And that fear of freedom will turn him into a slave of this power. For this reason, the jewels are evil. That is why we have summoned you to steal them from us."

"To steal them from you?" asked Geo. "Why couldn't you have simply destroyed them when you had them?"

"We have already been infected." The god smiled. "We are a small number here on Aptor. To reach this state of organization, to collect the scattered scientific knowledge of the times before the Great Fire, was not easy. Too often the jewels have been used, and abused, and now we cannot destroy them. We would have to destroy ourselves, first. We kidnapped Argo and left you the second jewel, hoping that you would come after the third and last one. Now you have come, and now the jewel is being stolen."

"Snake?" asked Geo.

"That's right," replied Hama.

"But I thought he was your spy," Geo said.

"That he is our spy is his unconscious reason for his actions," explained Hama. "He is aware only that he is working against the evil he has seen in Jordde. Spy is too harsh a word for him. Say, rather, little thief. He became a spy for us quite unwittingly when he was on the Island as a child with Jordde. I have explained something to you of how the mind works. We have machines that can duplicate what Snake does in a similar way that the jewels work. This is how the blind priestesses contacted Jordde and made him their spy. This is how we reached Snake. But he never saw us, never even really talked to us. It was mainly because of something he saw, something he saw when he first got here.''

"Wait a minute," Iimmi said. "Jordde wanted to kill me, and he did kill Whitey, because of something we saw here. It must have been the same thing. But what was it?''

Hama smiled. "My telling you would do no good. Perhaps you can find out from Snake, or my daughter, Argo Incarnate.''

"But what do we do now?'' Geo interrupted. "Take the jewels back to Argo? I mean Argo on the ship. She's already used the jewels to control minds, at least Snake's, so that means she's 'infected' too.''

"Once, you guessed the reason for her 'infection,' '' said Hama. "We have been watching you on our screens since you landed. Do you remember what the reason was?''

"Do you mean her being jealous of her daughter?'' Geo asked.

"Yes. On one side her motives were truly patriotic for Leptar. On the other hand they were selfish ones of power seeking. But without the selfish ones, she would have never gotten so far as she did. You must bring young Argo back and give the infection a chance to work itself out.''

"But what about the jewels?'' asked Geo. "All three of them will be together. Isn't that a huge temptation?''

"Someone must meet this temptation, and overcome it,'' said Hama. "You do not know the danger they create while they are here in Aptor.''

Hama turned to the screen and pushed a switch to "on'' position. The opaque glass filled with a picture of the interior of the Temple. On the great statue, a spotlight followed two microscopic figures over the statue's shoulder. They climbed over the statue's elbow.

Hama increased the size. The two made their way along the statue's forearm, to the golden stalks of wheat in the god's black fist. One after the other they shimmed down the stem. At the base they climbed over the rail. The view enlarged again.

"It's Snake!'' said Geo.

"And he's got the jewel!'' Urson added.

"That's Argo with him," Iimmi put in. "I mean . . . one of the Argos." They gathered around the screen to watch the congregation give way before the frightened children. Argo held onto Snake's shoulder.

Suddenly Hama turned the picture off. They looked away from the screen, puzzled. "So you see," said the god, "the jewel has been stolen. For the sake of Argo, and of Hama, carry the jewels back to Leptar. Young Argo will help you. Though we here are pained to see her go, she is as prepared for the journey as you are, if not more. Will you do it?"

"I will," Iimmi said.

"Me too," said Geo.

"I guess so," Urson said.

"Good," smiled Hama. "Then come with me." He turned from the screen and walked through the door. They followed him down the long stairway, past the stone walls, into the hall, and along the back of the church. He walked slowly, and smiled like a man who had waited long for something finally come. They left the Temple and descended the bright steps.

"I wonder where the kids are," Urson said.

Hama led them across the garden. Black urns sat close in the shrubbery. Old Argo joined them at the crosswalk with a silent smile of recognition. They turned from the path and stepped between the urns.

Argo twisted two ends of wire together with sun-dappled hands. Snake, knees beneath his arms, set the jewel on the improvised thermo-couple. Now Argo crouched too. They concentrated at the bead. The thermo-couple glowed: current jumped in the copper veins, the metal core became a magnet, and the armature tugged once about its pivot, tugged once more. Brushes hissed on the turning rings. The coil whirled to copper haze. "Hey!" she whispered. "Look at it go, will you! Just look at that thing go!" Oblivious to the elder gods, who smiled at them from the sides of the stone urn, the young thieves gazed at the humming motor.

CHAPTER ELEVEN

Under the trees, she stood on tiptoe and kissed the Priest's balding forehead. "Dunderhead," she said, "I think you're cute." Then she blinked rapidly and knuckled beneath her eye. "Oh," she added, remembering, "I was making yogurt in the biology laboratory yesterday. There's two gallons of it fermenting under the tarantula cage. Remember to take it out. And take care of the hamsters. Please don't forget the hamsters!"

That was the last of some twenty or twenty-five good-byes. There had been the entrusting of the shell collection, several exchanges of poems, the confession of authorship to a dozen practical jokes, and again respects to old Argo and Hama.

They started along the slope of the volcano. The Temple disappeared among the trees behind.

"Two days to get to the ship." Geo squinted at the pale sky.

"Perhaps we had better put the jewels together," said Urson. "Keep them out of harm's way, since we know their power."

"What do you mean?" Iimmi asked.

Urson took the leather purse from Geo's belt. "Give me your jewel."

Geo hesitated, then he took the thong from his neck; Urson put it in the purse.

"I guess it can't hurt," Iimmi said, and dropped his chain after it.

"Here's mine too," Argo said. She had been carrying the third one. She had woven the cord she used to climb the

statue into a small net sack, put the jewel inside, and hung it
around her neck. Now she gave it to him.

Urson pulled the purse string and tucked the pouch at his
waist.

"Well," said Geo, "I guess we head for the river, so
we can get back to your mother and Jordde."

"Jordde?" asked Argo. "Who's he?"

"He's a spy for the blind priestesses. He's also the one
who cut Snake's tongue out."

"Cut his . . . ?" Suddenly she stopped. "That's right:
four arms, his tongue—I remember now, in the film!"

"In the what?" asked Iimmi. "What do you remember?"

Argo turned to Snake. "I remember where I saw you
before!"

"You know Snake?" Urson asked.

"No. I never met him. But about a month ago I saw a
movie of what happened. It was horrible what they did to
him."

"What's a movie?" asked Iimmi.

"Huh?" said Argo. "Oh, it's sort of like the vision
screens, only you can see things that happened in the past.
Anyway, Dunderhead showed me this film about a month
ago. Then he took me down to the beach and said I should
have seen something there, because of what I'd learned."

"See something! What was it?" He took her shoulder
and shook it. "What was it you were supposed to see?"

"Why . . . ?" began the girl, startled.

"Because a friend of mine was murdered and I almost
was, too, because of something we saw on that beach! Only I
don't know what it was!"

"But . . ." began Argo. "But I don't either. I couldn't
see it, so Dunderhead took me back to the Temple."

"Snake?" Geo asked. "Do you know what they were
supposed to see? Or why Argo was taken to see it after she
was shown what happened to you?"

The boy shrugged.

Iimmi turned on Snake. "Do you know, or are you just
not telling? Come on now! That's the only reason I stuck with
this so far. I want to know what's going on!"

Snake shook his head.

"I want to know why I was nearly killed!" the black sailor insisted. "You know and I want you to tell me!" Iimmi raised his hand.

Snake screamed. Sound tore through the distended vocal cords. Then he whirled and ran.

Urson caught him and brought the boy crashing down among leaves. "No you don't!" the giant growled. "You're not going to get away from me this time."

"Watch out!" cried Argo. "You're hurting him. Urson, let go!"

"Hey, ease up," said Geo. "Snake, you've got to give us some explanation. Let him go, Urson."

Urson let the boy up, still mumbling. "He's not going to get away again."

Geo came over to the boy. "Let him go. Look, Snake, do you know what there was about the beach that was so important?"

Snake nodded.

"Can you tell?"

Now the boy shook his head and glanced at Urson.

"You don't have to be afraid of him," Geo said, puzzled. "Urson won't hurt you."

But Snake shook his head again.

"Well," said Geo, "we can't make you. Let's get going."

"I could make him," Urson mumbled.

"No," said Argo. "I don't think you could. I watched the last time somebody tried. And I don't think you could."

Late morning flopped over hot in the sky, turning to afternoon. The jungle grew damp. Bright insects plunged like tiny knives of blue or scarlet through the foliage. Wet leaves brushed their chests, faces, and shoulders.

At the edge of a rocky stretch, Urson suddenly drew his sword and hacked at a shadow which resolved into a medium-sized cat-like animal. Blood ran over the rock and mixed with encrusted leaves in the dirt.

No one suggested using the jewels for fire. As Iimmi was striking stones over a handful of tinder, he suddenly asked, "Why would they show you a film of something awful before taking you to the beach?"

"Maybe it was supposed to have made me more receptive to what I saw," said Argo.

"If horror makes you receptive to whatever it was," said Iimmi, "I should have been about as receptive as possible."

"What do you mean?" asked Geo.

"I had just watched ten guys get hacked to pieces all over the sand, remember?" The fire flickered, caught, and held.

As they ate, Argo got out a packet of salt from her tunic, then disappeared with Snake into the woods, to come back two minutes later with a purplish vine which she said made good spice when the bark was stripped and the pith rubbed on meat. "Back at the Temple," she told them, sitting down in front of the fire, "I had a great herb garden. There was one whole section for poisonous plants: Death Angel, Wolfsbane, Deadly Nightshade, Monk's Hood, Hebenon, the whole works." She laughed. Then the laugh stopped. "I guess I won't be going back there again. For a little while, anyway." She twisted the vine. "It was a beautiful garden, though." Then she let the stem untwist.

They left the rocky plateau for lower woods, and the dampness grew and the light lessened. "Are you sure we're going the right way?" Urson asked.

"It should be," said Iimmi.

"It is," said Argo. "We'll come out at the head of the river. It's a huge marsh that drains off into the main channel."

Evening came quickly.

"I was wondering about something," Geo said, after a little while.

"What?" asked Argo.

"Hama said that once the jewels had been used to control minds, the person who used them was infected. . . ."

"Rather the infection was already there," corrected Argo. "That just brought it out."

"Yes," said Geo. "Anyway, Hama also said that he was infected. When did he have to use the jewels?"

"Lots of times," Argo said. "Too many. The last time was when I was kidnapped. He used the jewel to control pieces of that thing you all killed in the City of New Hope to come and kidnap me and then leave the jewel in Leptar."

"A piece of that monster?" Geo exclaimed. "No wonder it decayed so rapidly when it was killed."

"Huh?" asked Iimmi.

"Argo—I mean your mother—told me they had managed to kill one of the kidnappers, and it melted the moment
it died."

"We couldn't control the whole mass," she explained.
"It really doesn't have a mind. But, like everything alive, it
has, or had, the double impulse."

"But what did kidnapping you accomplish, anyway?"
Iimmi asked.

Argo grinned. "It brought you here. And now you're
taking the jewels away."

"Is that all?" asked Iimmi.

"Well, jeepers," said Argo. "Isn't that enough?" She
paused for an instant. "You know, I wrote a poem about all
this once, the double impulse and everything."

Geo recited:

> "*By the dark chamber sits its twin,*
> *where the body's floods begin,*
> *and the two are twinned again,*
> *turning out and turning in.*"

"How did you know?"

"The dark chamber is Hama's Temple," Geo said. "Am
I right?"

"And its twin is Argo's," she went on. "They should
be twins, really. And then the twins again are the children.
The force of age in each one opposed to the young force.
See?"

"I see," Geo smiled. "And the body's floods, turning
in and out?"

"That's sort of everything man does, his going and
coming, his great ideas, his achievements, his little ideas,
too. It all comes from the interplay of those four forces."

"Four?" said Urson. "I thought it was just two."

"But it's thousands!" Argo exclaimed.

"It's too complicated for me," said Urson. "How far do
we have to go to the river?"

"We should be there by evening," Iimmi calculated.

"And we're headed right," Argo assured them again. "I think."

"One more thing," asked Geo. The ground beneath the fallen leaves was black and spongy now. "How did your grandmother get to Aptor?"

"By helicopter," Argo said.

"By what?" asked Iimmi.

"It's like a very small ship that flies in the air, and it goes much faster than a boat in water."

"I didn't mean the method of transportation," said Geo.

"When she had decided her daughter was reigning steadily in Leptar, she just went to Aptor permanently. I didn't even know about it until I was kidnapped. I've learned a lot since I came here."

"I guess we have, too," said Geo. "But there's still that one thing more, at the beach."

"Then let's hurry up and get there," said Urson. "We're slowing down, and we don't have much time."

The air was almost drenched. The leaves had been shiny before. Now they dripped water on the loose ground. Pale light lapsed through the branches, shimmered from leaf to the wet underside of leaf. The ground became mud.

Twice they heard a sloshing a few feet away, and then the scuttling of an unseen animal. "I hope I don't step on something that decides to take a chunk out of my foot."

"I'm pretty good at first aid," Argo said. "I'm getting chilly," she added.

Urson *humphed* now as the trees thinned around them. The muddy forest floor for yards at a span was coated with water that became mirrors for the trees stuck in its surface.

"Start watching out for quicksand," Geo said. They went more cautiously now. "Just keep within grabbing distance of a tree."

"They're getting sort of far apart," said Argo.

Just then, Geo, who was a bit ahead of the others, cried out. When they reached him he had already sunk knee-deep. He threw himself to the side and his good arm wrapped around the trunk of a thin black tree. He tried to grab on with his nub too, but he just scraped it on the bark.

"Hold on!" Urson called. He skirted the pool, and

grabbed the trunk of the tree with one hand and Geo with the other. Geo came up, coated to the thigh with gray. As Urson helped him to more solid ground, the tree which they had grabbed suddenly tilted, and then splashed forward in a medusa of roots. A nameless animal slithered from the matted, dripping stalks. Then the whole thing slipped beneath the mud and there were only ripples.

"You all right?" Urson still supported him. "You sure you're all right?"

Geo nodded, rubbing the stump of his arm with his good hand. "I'm all right," he said. They gathered together and began once more through the mud. The trees gave out.

Geo suddenly saw the whole swamp shiver in front of him. He splashed a step backwards, but Urson caught his shoulder. Ripples appeared over the water, spreading, crossing, webbing the whole surface with a net of tiny waves.

And they rose: green backs broke the water. They stood now, torrents cascading their green faces, green chests. Three of them, now a fourth. Four more, then many more. Their naked bodies were mottled green.

Geo felt a sudden tugging in his head, at his mind. Looking around he saw that the others felt it too.

"Them . . ." Urson started.

"They're the ones who . . . carried us . . ." Geo began. The tug came again, and they stepped forward. He put his hand on his head. "They want . . . us to go with them. . . ." And suddenly he was going forward, slipping into the familiar state of half-consciousness which had come when he had crossed the river, to the City of New Hope, or when he had first fallen into the sea.

Wet hands fell on their bodies and guided them through the swamp. They were carried through deeper water. Now they were walked over dry land where the vegetation was thicker. Slimy boulders caught shards of sunset on their wet flanks.

Dripping canopies of moss looped the branches. Water rose to their knees, their stomachs, their necks. A bright wash of pebbles and shells resolved through the water, as if their eyes had been pushed close to the sea bottom, sensitized to new light. The air was white, static, and electric. Then it slipped through blue to black. There were red eyes in the blackness. Through a rip in the arras of vegetation, they saw the moon push between the clouds, staining them silver. A rock rose against the moonlight where a naked man stared at the white disk. As they passed, he howled (or anyway, opened his mouth and threw his head back. But their ears were full of night and could not hear) and dropped to all fours. A breeze blew in the sudden plume of his tail, in the scraggly hair of his underbelly, and light lay white on the points of his ears, his lengthened muzzle, his thinned hind legs. He turned his head once, and scampered down the rock and into the darkness. A curtain of trees swung across the open sky. Eyes of flame glittered ahead of them. Water swirled their knees once more, then went down. Sand washed from beneath their feet along the dark beach. The beating of the sea, the rush of the river. Wet leaves fingered their cheeks, tickled their shins, and slapped their bellies as they moved forward. All fell away.

Light flickered on the wet rocks as they entered the largest cave. Their eyes focused once more. Foam washed back and forth over the sandy floor, and black chains of weeds caught in crevices on the stone, twisted on the sand with the inrush of water. Webbed hands released them.

Brown rocks rose around them in the firelight. They raised their eyes to a rock throne where the Old One sat. His long spines were strung with shrunken membranes. His eyes, gray and clouded, were close to the surface of his broad-nostriled face. Water trickled over the rock where he sat. Others stood about him.

They glanced at one another. Outside the cave it was raining hard. Argo's hair, wet to dark auburn, hugged her head, with little streaks down her neck.

A voice boomed at them, with more than just the natural sonority of the cave: "Carriers of the jewels," it began. Geo realized that it was the same hollowness that accompanied Snake's soundless messages. "We have brought you here to give a warning. We are the oldest forms of intelligence on this planet. We have watched from the delta of the Nile the rise of the pyramids; we have seen the murder of Caesar from the banks of the Tiber. We watched the Spanish Armada destroyed by England, and we followed Man's great metal fish through the ocean before the Great Fire. We have never aligned ourselves with either Argo or Hama, but rise in the sexless swell of the ocean. We come only to touch men when they are bloated with death. You have carried, and used, the jewels of Aptor, the Eyes of Hama, the Treasure of Argo, the Destroyers of Reason, the playthings of children. Whether you use them to control minds, or to make fire, all carriers of the jewels are maimed. But we can warn you, as we have warned Man before. As before, some will listen, some will not. Your minds are your own, that I pledge you. Now I warn you: cast the jewels into the sea.

"Nothing is ever lost in the sea, and when the evil has been washed from them with time and brine, they will be returned to you. For then time and brine will have washed away your imperfections also.

"No living intelligence is free from their infection, nothing with the double impulse of life. But we are old, and can hold them for a million years before we will be so infected as you are. Your young race is too condensed in its living to tolerate such power in its fingers now. Again I say: cast them into the sea.

"The knowledge which man needs to alleviate hunger and pain from the world is contained in two temples on this Island. Both have the science to put the jewels to use, to the good use which is possible with them. Both have been infected. In Leptar, however, where you carry these jewels, there is no way at all to utilize them for anything but evil. There will be only the temptation to destroy."

"What about me?" Argo piped up. "I can teach them all sorts of things in Leptar." She took one of Snake's hands. "We used one for our motor."

"You will find something else to make your motor run. You still have to recognize something that you have already seen."

"At the beach?" demanded Iimmi.

"Yes." the Old One nodded, with something like a sigh. "At the beach. We have a science that allows us to do things which to you seem impossibilities, as when we carried you in the sea for weeks without your body decaying. We can enter your mind as Snake does. And we can do much else.

We have a wisdom which far surpasses even Argo's and Hama's on Aptor. Will you cast the jewels into the sea and trust them with us?''

"How can we give you the jewels?" Urson demanded: "First of all, how can we be sure you're not going to use them against Argo and Hama once you get them? You say nobody is impervious to them. And we've only got your say-so on how long it would take you to fall victim. You can already influence minds. That's how you got us here. And according to Hama, that's what corrupts. And you've already done it."

"Besides," Geo said. "There's something else. We've nearly messed this thing up a dozen times trying to figure out motives and counter-motives. And it always comes back to the same thing: we've got a job to do, and we ought to do it. We're supposed to return Argo and the jewels to the ship, and that's what we're doing."

"He's right," said Iimmi. "Rule Number One again: Act on the simplest theory that holds all the information."

The Old One sighed a second time. "Once, fifteen hundred years ago, a man who was to maneuver one of the metal birds that was to drop fire from the sky walked and pondered by the sea. He had been given a job to do. We tried to warn him, as we tried to warn you. But he jammed his hands into the pockets of his uniform, and uttered to the waves the words you just uttered, and the warning was shut out of his mind. He scrambled up over the dunes on the beach, never taking his hands out of his pockets. He drank one more cup of coffee that night than usual. The next morning, at five o'clock, when the sun slanted red across the air field, he climbed into his metal bird, took off, flew for some time over the sea, looking down on the water like crinkled foil under the heightening sun, until he reached land again. Then he did his job: he pressed a button which released two shards of fire metal in a housing of cobalt. The land flamed. The sea boiled in the harbors. And two weeks later he was also dead. That which burned your arm away, Poet, burned his whole face away, boiled his lungs in his chest and his brain in his skull." There was a pause. "Yes, we can control minds. We could have relieved the tiredness, immobilized the fear, the terror, immobilized all his unconscious reasons for doing what he did, just as man can now do with the jewels. But had we, we would have also immobilized the . . . humanity he clung to. Yes, we can control minds, but we do not." The voice swelled. "But never, since that day on the shore before the Great Fire, has the temptation to do so been as great as now." The voice returned to normal. "Perhaps," and there was almost humor in it now. "Perhaps you are right. Perhaps the temptation is too great, even for us. Perhaps we have reached the place where the jewels would push us just across the line we have never crossed before, make us do those things that we have never done." Another pause. "There, you have heard our warning now. The choice, I swear to you, is yours."

They stood silent in the high cave, the fire on their faces weaving brightness and shadow. Geo turned to look at the rain-blurred darkness outside the cave.

"Out there is the sea," said the voice again. "Your decision quickly. The tide is coming in. . . ."

It was snatched from their minds before they could articulate it. Two children saw a bright motor turning in the shadow. Geo and Iimmi saw the temples of Argo in Leptar. Then there was something darker, from Urson. And for a moment, they all saw all the pictures at once. And then they were gone.

"Very well, then," boomed the voice. "Keep them!"

A wave splashed across the floor, like twisted glass before the rock on which the fire stood. Then it flopped wetly across the burning driftwood. They were hissed into darkness. Charred sticks turned, glowing in the water, and were extinguished.

Rain was buffeting them, hands held them once more, pulling them into the warm sea, the darkness, and then nothing. . . .

Snake was thinking again, and this time through the Captain's eyes:

The cabin door burst open in the rain. Her wet veils whipped about the door frame; lightning made them transparent. Jordde rose from his seat. She closed the door on thunder.

I have received the signal from the sea, *she said.* Tomorrow you pilot the ship into the estuary.

The Captain's voice: But, Priestess Argo, I cannot take the ship into Aptor. We already have lost ten men; I cannot sacrifice . . .

And the storm, *Jordde smiled. If it is like this tomorrow, how can I take her through the rocks?*

Her nostrils flared; her lips compressed to a chalky line. She regarded Jordde.

The Captain's thoughts: What is between them, this confused tension. It upsets me deeply, and I am tired. . . .

You will pilot the boat to shore tomorrow, *Argo hissed.* They have returned, with the jewels!

The Captain's thoughts: They speak to each other in a code I don't understand. I am so tired, now. I have to protect my ship, my men; that is my job, my responsibility.

Argo turned to the Captain. Captain, I hired you to obey me. You promised this when you took my commission, and you knew it involved danger in Aptor. You must order your Mate to pilot this ship to Aptor's shore tomorrow morning.

The Captain's thoughts: Yes, yes. The fatigue and the unknowing. But I must fulfill, must complete . . . Jordde, he began.

Yes, Captain, *answered the Mate, anticipating.* If the weather is permitting, sir, I will take the ship as close as I can get. *He smiled a thin curve over his face, and looked back at Argo.*

CHAPTER TWELVE

Roughness of sand beneath one of his sides, and the flare of the sun on the other. His eyes were hot and his lids orange over them. He turned over, and reached out to dig his hands into the sand. One hand closed.

He opened his eyes, and rolled to his knees. The sand grated under his kneecaps. Looking out toward the water, he saw that the sun hung only inches above the horizon. Then he saw the ship.

It was heading toward the estuary of the river down the beach. He stood up and looked around. He was alone. The estuary was to his left. He began to run toward where the rocks and vegetation cut off the end of the beach. The sand under his feet was cool.

A moment later he saw Iimmi's dark figure run from the jungle, heading for the same place. Geo hailed him. Panting, they joined each other. Together they continued toward the rocks.

As they broke through the first foliage, they nearly bumped into red-haired Argo, who stood, knuckling her eyes, in the shadow of the broad palm fronds. When she recognized them, she joined them silently. Finally they reached the outcropping of rocks a few hundred feet up the river bank.

The rain had swelled the river's mouth to tremendous violence. It vomited brown water into the ocean, frothed against rocks, and boiled opaquely below them. It was nearly half again as wide as Geo remembered it.

Although the sky was clear, beyond the brown bile of the river, the sea snarled viciously and bared its white teeth to the early sun. It took another fifteen minutes for the boat to maneuver through granite spikes toward the rocky embankment.

Staring down into the turbulence, Argo whispered, "So fast . . ." But that was the only human sound against the roar.

The boat's prow doffed in the swell. At last her plank swung out and bumped unsteadily on the rocks. Figures were gathering on deck.

"Hey," Argo said, pointing toward one. "That's Mom!"

"Where the hell are Snake and Urson?" Iimmi asked.

"That's Snake down there," Geo said. "Look!" He pointed with his nub.

Snake crouched near the gangplank itself. He was behind a ledge of rock, hidden from the people on the ship, but plain to Geo and his companions.

Geo said: "I'm going down there. You stay here." He ducked through the vines, keeping in sight of the rocks' edge and the boiling foam. He reached a sheltered rise, just ten feet above the nest of rock in which the four armed boy was crouching.

Geo looked out at the boat. Jordde stood at the head of the gangplank. The eighteen feet of board was unsteady with the roll of the ship. Jordde held a black whip in his hand, only the end went to a box strapped to his back. With the lash raised, he stepped onto the shifting plank.

Geo wondered what the contrivance was. The answer came with the hollow sound of Snake's thoughts:

that . . . is . . . machine . . . he . . . used . . . to . . . cut . . . tongue . . . with . . . only . . . on . . . whip . . . not . . . wire . . . So Snake knew he was just behind him. As he tried to understand exactly the implications of what Snake had said, suddenly, with the speed of a bird's shadow, Snake leaped from his hiding place and landed on the end of the plank, recovered from his crouch, and rushed out toward Jordde, apparently intending to knock him from the board.

Jordde raised the lash and it fell across the boy's shoulder. It didn't land hard; it just dropped. But Snake reeled, and went down on one knee, grabbing the sides of the plank. Geo was close enough to hear the boy scream.

"I cut your tongue out once with this thing," Jordde said matter-of-factly. "Now I'm going to cut the rest of you to pieces." He adjusted a control at his belt and raised the lash again—

Geo leaped for the plank. The sudden swell of anger and fear defined the action, but once on the end of the plank, facing Jordde over crouching Snake, he wondered how wise it had been. Then he had to stop wondering and try to duck the falling lash. He couldn't.

It landed with only the weight of gravity, brushing his cheek, then dropping across his shoulder and down his back. He screamed: it felt like the whole side of his face had been seared away, and an inch deep crevice burned into his shoulder and back the whole length it touched him. He bit white fire, trying not to leap aside into the foaming chasm between rocks and boat. As the lash rasped away, sweat flooded into his eyes. His good arm, which held the edge of the plank as he crouched, was shaking like a plucked string on a loose guitar. Snake staggered back against him, almost knocking him over. When Geo blinked the tears out of his eyes, he saw two bright welts on Snake's shoulder. Jordde stepped out on the plank, smiling.

When the line fell again, he wasn't sure just what happened. He leaned in one direction. Snake was a dive of legs in the other, then only four sets of fingers over the edge of the plank. Geo screamed again and shook.

Two sets of fingers disappeared from one side of the board and reappeared on the other. As Jordde raised the lash a fourth time to rid the plank of this one armed nuisance, the fingers worked rapidly forward toward Jordde's feet. An arm raised from beneath the plank, grabbed Jordde's ankle, and the lash fell far of Geo. He was still trembling, trying to move back off the unsteady plank, and keep from vomiting at the same time.

Jordde lost his balance, but turned in time to grab the rail of the ship's gate. At the same time, one leg, then the other, came over the side of the plank. Snake rolled to a crouch on top of the board.

Geo got his feet under him, and stumbled off the plank. Back on the rocks, he sat down, hard. He clutched his good arm across his stomach, and without lowering his eyes, leaned forward to cool his back.

Jordde, half-seated on the board, lashed the whip sideways. Snake leaped a foot as the line swung beneath his feet. All four arms went spidering out to regain equilibrium. The whip struck the side of the boat, left a burn on the hull, and came swinging back again. Snake leaped once more and made it.

Suddenly there was a shadow over Geo, and he saw Urson stride up to the end of the plank. Back to Geo, the big sailor crouched bear-like at the plank's head. "All right, now try someone a little bigger than you. Come on, kid; get off there. I want my turn." Urson's sword was drawn.

Snake turned, grabbed at something on Urson, but the big man knocked him away as he leaped diagonally onto the shore. Urson laughed over his shoulder. "You don't want the ones around my neck," he called back. "Here, keep these for me." He tossed Geo's leather purse from his belt back to the shore. Snake landed just as Jordde flung the lash out again. Urson must have caught the line across his chest, because his back suddenly stiffened. Then he leaped forward and came down with his sword so hard that had Jordde still been there, his leg would have been severed. Jordde leaped back onto the edge of the ship, and the sword sliced three inches into the wood. As Urson tried to pull the blade free Jordde sent his whip singing again. It wrapped Urson's midsection like a black serpent; and it didn't come loose.

Urson howled. He flung his sword forward. The blade sank inches through Jordde's abdomen. The Mate bent forward with a totally amazed expression, grabbed the line with both hands, and tugged backwards, screaming.

Jordde took two steps onto the plank, mouth open, eyes closed, and fell over the side.

Urson, without stopping his own howl or letting go of the line, heaved backwards, and toppled from the other side. For a moment they hung with the whip between them, over the board. The ship heaved back, and then rolled to. The plank swiveled, came loose; and, with the board on top of them, they crashed into the water.

Geo and Snake scrambled to the rocks' edge. Iimmi and Argo were coming up behind them.

Below them, the tangle of limbs and board bobbed in the foam once. The line had somehow looped around Urson's eck, and the plank had turned up almost on end. They went under again.

With nothing between it and the rocky shore, the boat began to roll in. With each swell, it came in six feet, and then leaned out three. Then it came back another six. It took four swells, the time of four very deep breaths, until the side of the boat was grating up against the rocks. Geo could hear the plank splintering in the water.

But the river's rush blanketed anything else that was breaking.

Geo took two steps backwards, clutched at his stubbed arm, and threw up from pain and terror.

Somebody, the Captain, was calling. "Get her away from the rocks! Away from the rocks, before she goes to pieces!"

Iimmi took Geo's arm. "Come on, boy!" He managed to haul him onto the ship. Argo and Snake leaped on behind them. The boat floundered away from the shore.

Geo leaned against the rail. Below him the water turned on itself in the rocks, thrashed along the river's side, and then, as he raised his eyes, stretched out along the bright blade of the beach. The long sand that rimmed the Island dropped away from them, a stately and austere arc gathering in its curve all the sun's glare, and throwing it back in wave, and on wave.

His back hurt, his stomach was shriveled and shaken like an old man's palsied fist, his arm was gone, and Urson . . . "Captain," Geo said. He turned from the rail, his good hand going to his nub. Then he bawled, "Captain!"

The little redhead caught his shoulder. "It . . . it won't do any good!"

"Captain!" he called again.

The elderly, gray-eyed man approached him. "What is it?"

He looks tired, Geo thought. *I'm tired.*

Iimmi was by his shoulder now. Geo was quiet, until Iimmi said, "Never mind, sir. I don't think you can do anything now."

"Are you sure?" the Captain asked, looking at the shocked black hair, the bruised face, the deep eyes. "Are you . . ."

"Never mind," Geo said. He turned back to the rail Below them, splinters of the plank were still washing up t the boat's hull and falling back into the white froth. Onl splinters. Only . . .

Then Argo said, "Look at the beach!"

Geo flung his eyes up and tried in one moment t envelope whatever he saw, whatever it would be. Beneath th water's roar was a still tide of quiet. The pale sand along th naked crescent was dull at some depressions, mirror bright a certain rises. At the jungle's edge, leaves and fronds spe multi-textured green rippling along the foliage-heavy limbs Each single fragment in that green tapestry hung up in th sun was one leaf, he reflected, with two sides, an entir system of skeleton and veins, as his arm had been. An maybe one day would drop off, too. He looked from rock t rock now. Each one was different, shaped and lined distinctly but losing detail as the ship floated further out, like th memory of his entire adventure was losing detail. That on there was like a bull's head half submerged; those two fla ones together on the sand looked like the stretched wings o eagles. And the waves, measured and magnificent, followe one another onto the sand, like the varying, never duplicate rhythm of a good poem: yet peaceful, ordered, and calm. H tried to pour the chaos of Urson's drowning from his mind ont the water. It flowed into each glass-green trough that rode u to the still beach. He tried to spread the pain in his own bod over the web of foam and shimmering green. And wa surprised because it fit so easily, hung there so well. Somewhere a very real understanding was beginning to effloresce with the sea's water, under the heightening sun.

Geo turned away from the rail. The wet deck slippe under his bare feet. He walked back toward the forecastle He had released his broken limb, now, and his hand hung a his side while he walked.

Later in the evening, he came on deck again. The veile Priestess stood by the railing. When he approached, sh turned to him and said quietly, "I did not want to disturb yo for a report until you had rested some."

"I've rested," he said. "We've returned your daughte to you, whether you like it or not. You can get the jewels from

Snake. He'll give them to you now. You can get your daughter
to explain everything about Hama."

"She has already," answered the Priestess, smiling.
"You've done very well, Poet, and bravely."

"Thanks," Geo said. Then he turned back to the forecastle.

When Snake came down that evening, Geo was lying on
his back in the bunk, following the grain of the wood on the
bottom of the bed above his. His good arm was behind his
neck now. Snake touched Geo's shoulder.

"What is it?" Geo asked, turning on his side and
looking from under the bunk.

Snake held out the leather purse to Geo.

"Huh?" Geo asked. "Didn't you give them to Argo
yet?"

Snake nodded.

"Well, why didn't she take them? Look, I don't want to
see them again."

Snake pushed the purse toward him again, and added:
look . . .

Geo took the purse, opened the drawstring, and turned
the contents out in his hand: there were three chains. On each
a gold coin was fastened by a hole near the edge. Geo
frowned. "How come these are in here?" he asked. "I
thought . . . where are the jewels?"

in . . . ocean . . . Snake said. *Urson . . . switched . . . them . . .*

"What are you talking about?" demanded Geo. "What
is it?"

don't . . . want . . . tell . . . you . . .

"I don't care what you want, you little bastard!" Geo
grabbed him by the shoulder. "Tell me!"

*know . . . from . . . back . . . with . . . blind . . . priestesses
. . .* Snake explained rapidly. *he . . . ask . . . me . . . how . . .
to . . . use . . . jewels . . . when . . . you . . . and . . . Iimmi . . .
exploring . . . and . . . after . . . that . . . no . . . listen . . . to . . .
thoughts . . . bad . . . thoughts . . . bad . . .*

"But he . . ." Geo started. "He saved your life!"

but . . . what . . . is . . . reason . . . Snake said. *at . . . end . . .*

"You saw his thoughts at the end?" asked Geo. "What
did he think?"

you . . . sleep . . . please . . . Snake said. *lot . . . of . . . hate . . . lot of . . . bad . . . hate . . .* There was a pause in the voice in his head. *and . . . love . . .*

Geo began to cry. A bubble of sound in the back of his throat burst, and he turned onto the pillow and tried to bite through the sound with his teeth, and tried to know why he was crying; for the tiredness, for the fear, for Urson, for his arm, and for the inevitable growth which hurt so much . . . his body ached; his back hurt in two sharp lines, and he couldn't stop crying.

Iimmi, who had taken the bunk above Geo's, came back a few minutes after mess. Geo had not felt like eating.

"How's your stomach?' Iimmi asked.

"Funny,'' Geo said. "But better, I guess.''

"Good,'' said Iimmi. "Food sort of weights you down, once it gets inside; sort of holds you down to earth.''

"I'll eat something soon,'' Geo said. He paused. "Now I guess you'll never find out what you saw on the beach that made you dangerous.'' The slosh of water on the hull outside was just audible; they were veering toward Leptar now.

Then Iimmi laughed. "I found what it was.''

"How?'' asked Geo. "When? What was it?''

"Same time you did,'' Iimmi said. "I just looked. And then Snake explained the details of it to me later.''

"When?'' Geo repeated.

"I took a nap just before dinner and he went through the whole thing with me.''

"Then what was it you saw, we saw?''

"Well, first of all; do you remember what Jordde was before he was shipwrecked on Aptor?''

"Didn't Argo say he was studying to be a priest? Old Argo, I mean.''

"Right,'' said Iimmi. "Now, do you remember what your theory was about what we saw?''

"Did I have a theory?' Geo asked.

"About horror and pain making you receptive to whatever it was.''

"Oh, that,'' Geo said. "I remember. Yes.''

"You were also right about that. Now add to all this

some theory from Hama's lecture on the double impulse of life: sift together; mix well. It wasn't a thing we saw; it was a situation, or rather an experience we had. Also, it didn't have to be on the beach. It could have happened anywhere. Man, with his constantly diametric motivations, is always trying to reconcile opposites. Take Hama's theory one step further: each action *is* a reconciliation of the duality of his motivation. Now, take all we've been through, the confusion, the pain, the disorder; reconcile that with the great order obvious in something like the sea, with its rhythm, its tides and waves, its overpowering calm, or the ordering of cells in a leaf, or a constellation of stars. If you can do it, something happens to you: you grow. You become a bigger person, able to understand, or reconcile, more."

"All right," said Geo.

"And that's what we saw, or the experience we had when we looked at the beach from the ship this morning; chaos caught in order, the order defining chaos."

"All right again," Geo said. "And I'll even assume that Jordde knew that the two impulses of this experience were something terrible and confused, like seeing ten men hacked to pieces by vampires, or seeing a film of a little boy getting his tongue pulled out, or coming through what we came through since we landed on Aptor, as well as something calm and ordered, like the beach and the sea. Now, why would he want to kill someone simply because he might have gone through what amounts, I guess, to the basic religious experience?"

"You picked just the right word." Iimmi smiled. "Jordde was a novice in the not too liberal religion of Argo. Jordde and Snake had probably been through nearly as much on Aptor as we had. And they survived. And they also emerged from that jungle of horror onto that great arching rhythm of waves and sand. And they went through just what you and I and Argo went through. Little Argo, I mean. And it was just at that point when the blind priestesses of Argo made contact with Jordde. They did so by means of those vision screens we saw them with, which can receive sound and pictures from just about anyplace, but can also project, at least sound, to just about anywhere, too. In other words, right in the middle of this religious, or mystic, or whatever you want to call it, experience, a voice materialized out of thin air that claimed to be the voice of the Goddess. Have you any idea what this did to his mind?''

"I imagine it took all the real significance out of the whole thing,'' Geo said. "It would for me.''

"It did,'' said Iimmi. "Jordde wasn't what you'd call stable before that. If anything, this made him worse. It also stopped his mental functioning from working in the normal way. And Snake, who was reading his mind at the time, suddenly saw himself watching the terrifying sealing up process of a more or less active and competent, if not healthy, mind. He saw it again in Urson, slower this time. But the same thing. It's apparently a pretty stiff thing to watch from the inside. That's why he stopped reading Urson's thoughts. The idea of stealing the jewels for himself was slowly eating away the balance, the understanding, the ability to reconcile disparities, like the incident with the blue lizard; things like that, all of which were signs we didn't see. Snake contacted Hama by telepathy, almost accidentally. But Hama's information about the aims of the blind priestesses, to get the jewels for themselves, was something to hold onto for the boy: the second part of his impulse to serve Hama, the first part being the awful thing that had happened to Jordde's mind at contact with the blind priestesses.''

"Still, why did Jordde want to kill anybody who had experienced this, voice of god and all?''

"Because Jordde had by now managed to do what a static mind always does. Everything became equivocated with everything else. The situation, the beach, the whole thing suddenly meant for him the revelation of a concrete God. He knew that Snake had contacted something also, something which the blind priestesses told him was thoroughly evil, an enemy, a devil. On the raft, on the boat, he religiously tried to 'convert' Snake, till at last, in evangelical fury, he cut the boy's tongue out with the electric generator and the hot wire which the blind Priestess had given him before he left. Why did he want to get rid of anybody who had seen his beach, a sacred place to him by now? One, because the devils were too strong and he didn't want anybody else possessed by them; Snake had been too much trouble resisting conversion. And two, because he was jealous that someone else might have that moment of exaltation and hear the voice of the Goddess also.''

"In other words, he thought what happened to him and Snake was something supernatural, actually connected with the beach itself, and didn't want it to happen to anybody else.''

"That's right.'' Iimmi sat on the bunk's edge. "Which is sort of understandable. They didn't come in contact with any of the technology of Aptor, and so it might well have seemed that way.''

Geo leaned back. "I can see how the same thing almost . . . almost might have happened to me. If everything had been the same.''

Geo closed his eyes. Snake came down and took the top bunk; and when he slept, Snake told him of Urson, of his last thoughts, and surprisingly, things he mostly knew, about hate, a lot of hate, and about love.

Emerging from the forecastle the next morning, bright sunlight fell across his face. He had to squint. When he did so, he saw her sitting cross-legged on the stretched canvas tarpaulin in one of the suspended lifeboats.

"Hi up there,'' he called.

"Hi down there. How are you feeling?''

Geo shrugged.

Argo slipped her feet over the gunwale and, with paper bag in hand, dropped to the deck. She bobbed up next to his shoulder, grinned, and said, "Hey, come on back with me. I want to show you something.''

"Sure.'' He followed her.

"I bet you must be looking forward to school,'' she said as they walked. "You and Iimmi might turn up in some of the same classes, now that you know each other.''

"Maybe,'' said Geo.

"Gee, are you glum!'' She pulled a long face under short shocks of red hair.

"I hope Iimmi and I do get into some classes together,'' Geo said.

"That's more like it.'' Suddenly she looked serious. "Your arm is worrying you. Why?''

Geo shrugged again. "I don't feel like a whole person. I guess I'm not really a whole person.''

"Don't be silly," said Argo. "Besides, maybe Snake will let you have one of his. How are the medical facilities in Leptar?"

"I don't think they're up to anything like that."

"We did grafting of limbs back on Aptor," Argo said. "A most interesting way we got around the antibody problem too. You see—."

"But that was back in Aptor," Geo said. "This is the real world we're going into now."

"Maybe I can get a doctor from the Temple to come over." She shrugged. "And then, maybe I won't be able to."

"It's a pleasant thought," Geo said.

When they reached the back of the ship, Argo took out the contraption from the paper bag. "I salvaged this in my tunic. Hope I dried it off well enough last night."

"It's your motor," Geo said.

"Um-hum." She set it on a low set of lockers by the cabin back wall.

"How are you going to work it?" he asked. "It's got to have that stuff, electricity."

"There is more than one way to shoe a centipede," Argo assured him. She reached behind the locker and pulled up a strange gizmo of glass and wire. "I got the lens from mom," she explained. "She's awfully nice, really. She says I can have my own laboratory all to myself. And I said she could have all the politics, which I think was wise of me, considering. Don't you?" She bent over the contraption. "Now, this lens here focuses the sunlight—isn't it a beautiful day—focuses it on these here thermo-couples. I got the extra metal from the ship's smith. He's sweet. Hey, we're going to have to compare poems from now on. I mean I'm sure you're going to write a whole handful about all of this. I certainly am. Anyway, you connect it up here."

She fastened two wires to two other wires, adjusted the lens; the tips of the thermo-couple glowed beneath the glass. The armature tugged about its pivot.

Geo looked up to see Snake and Iimmi leaning over the rail on the cabin roof.

"Hey," Argo called. "Move out of the light!"

Grinning, they moved aside.

Brushes hissed on the turning rings. The coil whirled to copper haze. "Look at that thing go!" She stepped back, fists proudly on her hips. "Just look at that thing go!"

New York
February, 1962

ABOUT THE AUTHOR

SAMUEL R. DELANY, born April Fool's. Day, 1942, grew up in New York City's Harlem. His novels *Babel-17* and *The Einstein Intersection* both won Nebula Awards from the Science Fiction Writers of America, as have his short fictions *Aye, and Gomorrah* and *Time Considered as a Helix of Semi-Precious Stones* (which also took a Hugo Award during the World Science Fiction Convention at Heidelberg). His books include *The Jewels of Aptor, The Fall of the Towers, Nova, Driftglass* (short stories), *Dhalgren, Triton, Heavenly Breakfast* (nonfiction) and *Tales of Nevèrÿon*. With his wife, National Book Award-winning poet Marilyn Hacker, he co-edited the speculative fiction quarterly *Quark*. He also wrote, directed and edited the half-hour film *The Orchid*. In 1975 he was visiting Butler Chair Professor of English at the State University of New York at Buffalo. For the last half dozen years Delany and Hacker have lived between New York, San Francisco and London. They have one daughter.

OUT OF THIS WORLD!

That's the only way to describe Bantam's great series of science fiction classics. These space-age thrillers are filled with terror, fancy and adventure and written by America's most renowned writers of science fiction. Welcome to outer space and have a good trip!

FANTASY AND SCIENCE FICTION FAVORITES

Bantam brings you the recognized classics as well as the current favorites in fantasy and science fiction. Here you will find the beloved Conan books along with recent titles by the most respected authors in the genre.

☐	20931	NEBULA WINNERS FOURTEEN	$2.95
		Frederik Pohl	
☐	20527	SYZYGY Frederik Pohl	$3.50
☐	14343	WIND FROM THE ABYSS	$2.50
		Janet Morris	
☐	20672	DARKWORLD DETECTIVE	$2.50
		J. Michael Reeves	
☐	20281	WAR OF OMISSION Kevin O'Donnell	$2.50
☐	20488	THE HEROES OF ZARA	$2.50
		Guy Gregory	
☐	14428	LORD VALENTINE'S CASTLE	$2.95
		Robert Silverberg	
☐	20156	BABEL-17 Samuel R. Delany	$2.50
☐	20063	GATES OF HEAVEN Paul Preuss	$2.25
☐	20870	JEM Frederik Pohl	$2.95
☐	13837	CONAN & THE SPIDER GOD #5	$2.25
		de Camp & Pratt	
☐	13831	CONAN THE REBEL #6	$2.25
		Paul Anderson	
☐	14532	HIGH COUCH OF SILISTRA	$2.50
		Janet Morris	
☐	22804	DRAGONDRUMS Anne McCaffrey	$2.75
☐	22556	DRAGONSINGER Anne McCaffrey	$2.75
☐	22557	DRAGONSONG Anne McCaffrey	$2.75
☐	20914	MAN PLUS Frederik Pohl	$2.75
☐	14846	THE GOLDEN SWORD Janet Morris	$2.50
☐	20592	TIME STORM Gordon R. Dickson	$2.95

Buy them at your local bookstore or use this handy coupon for ordering: